Publisher's Note

The Windy Song is a work of fiction written by Ingo Swann in 1976.

For a long time, this work was a rather dusty collection of typewritten pages and handwritten notes, sitting in a box high upon a shelf in Swann's office. As the years went by, he would at times glance in the box's direction, wistfully, all the while leaning back in his chair, puffing away at a cigar, contemplating.

Serving as a transcendental channel to portraying timelessness and the psychological analogy of the heart, these pages are Swann's heartfelt narration about the meaning of memory and reincarnation.

Names, characters, businesses, places, events, locales, and incidents are either the products of Ingo Swann's imagination or used in a fictitious manner. Any resemblance to actual persons, living or dead, or actual events is purely coincidental.

We are extremely honored to publish this book in his memory.

Ingo Swann (1933-2013) was an American artist and exceptionally successful subject in parapsychology experiments. As a child he spontaneously had numerous paranormal experiences, mostly of the OBE type, the future study of which became a major passion as he matured. In 1970, he began acting as a parapsychology test subject in tightly controlled laboratory settings with numerous scientific researchers. Because of the success of most of these thousands of test trials, major media worldwide often referred to him as "the scientific psychic." His subsequent research on behalf of American intelligence interests, including that of the CIA, won him top PSI-spy status. His involvement in government research projects required the discovery of innovative approaches toward the actual realizing of subtle human energies.

He viewed PSI powers as only parts of the larger spectrum of human sensing systems and was internationally known as an advocate and researcher of the exceptional powers of the human mind.

To learn more about Ingo, his work, art, and other books, please visit: **www.ingoswann.com**.

THE WINDY SONG

A BioMind Superpowers Book
Published by

Swann-Ryder Productions, LLC
www.ingoswann.com

First edition BioMind Superpowers Books.

Cover art:
Reflection by Ingo Swann © Swann-Ryder Productions, LLC.

Internal art: Shutterstock.com
Retro Tree © Donovan van Staden
Retro Tree Blowing in the Wind © Donovan van Staden

ISBN-13: 978-1-949214-80-2

THE WINDY SONG

INGO SWANN

To Rebecca Alban Hoffberger
a special light in the universe

PRELUDE

Life is both the sun and the shadows.

In the early autumn, out on the Nebraskan prairies, a tiny girl child was born a few weeks before her natural time to enter life. This young child neither cried nor opened her eyes, on top of that, her breaths were short and weak. So frail, in fact, was her poor little body that everyone feared she wouldn't catch on to the life forces all babes must take hold of, if they are to live. This caused her mother's heart, and her father's, too, to ache with grief. Together this mother and father tried their best to comfort each other. Even so, they feared that this frail being, their first and only child, would quickly pass, vainly, into and out of life, without even opening her eyes.

Though, as fate would have it, this time of dread was dispatched, and the child opened her eyes -- eyes that would turn out to be big beyond imagination and of a color grey that was so immense that it gleamed a beautiful light.

At this, first the child's mother, then her father, too, witnessed this bold light, and a remarkable strength of life, being taken hold of by this being, their new and first daughter. As relief washed over them, first her mother cried the tears not of grief, but of great release, and then her father cried the same, although it wasn't thought manly among men in Nebraska to do so.

As her life forces now caught on, the child began to cry and bubble and wave her weak new arms, and, too, demanded feedings on time and when there were expected. With that, the time of untimely dread was quickly forgotten and there was perhaps an over-zealous flurry to see to this new babe's needs now that it happily seemed the parents' daughter was finally here to stay and for good.

Then, when her great relief was completed, and had turned into motherhood's joy and pride, the babe's mother thought to give the name of Alina to her new and first daughter because she had somewhere heard it meant "light" in one language or another, even if she wasn't exactly sure which language it was. "Just look, Richard," she said to her husband, "at her big, warm grey light-filled eyes. Let's call her Alina, and be glad this light welled up and stayed." What could her father do but agree, especially considering all the circumstances. So he said to his wife: "Julia, whatever you want is okay with me."

In this way, Alina came fitfully into her life in the autumn on the Nebraskan prairies where houses and farms were still placed far apart, but where friends were always near and true enough. Time moved on and twelve or so years passed, during which nothing else very unusual occurred…until the time when Alina slowly began approaching the first blushes of young womanhood, even though, as is not unusual, she was still thought of and treated as a young child, and indeed thought of herself that way.

It was at this mark, on the eve of her thirteenth birthday, a thing both of dread and wonder came upon Alina, for a deep memory in her loving soul opened its doors into another time which had passed not all that long ago.

Chapter
ONE

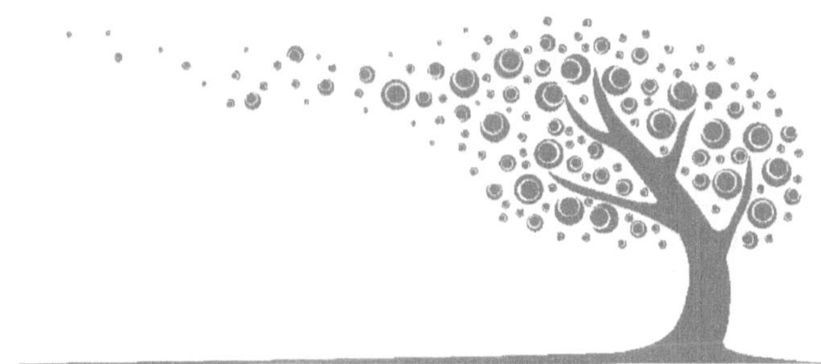

The Nebraska prairie winds didn't know which way to blow as was usual in that annual change between autumn and winter. The winds at this time came and went, first one way, and then another, sometimes billowing the clouds above, sometimes sweeping the earth below -- warm winds from the south, chilly winds from the north, toppling old and unsteady windmills and unhinging barn doors.

A body didn't know which way to lean, exactly. It was an irksome few weeks while everyone awaited the ultimate arrival of the true north winds, cold, dry, and full of winter.

Young Alina, though, loved this season, its winds blowing her long pale hair in all directions at once. Not that the shifting winds weren't fretful or even dangerous. There was always a chance of late autumnal tornados. Yet, if some gritted their teeth in expectation of the long winter coming, Alina's blood rose into new life. She knew she had been born at the time of these fretful winds. It was among them that her soul had found how to steady itself. Each year since, she had come to experience renewing happiness with her hold on life.

Also, and much to her great thrill, she always *grew* during the autumn, her genetic coding responding to signals different than those of other children who grew mostly at spring.

She loved the feeling of growing, the feeling of getting older, and each autumnal shift indicated that womanhood was one year closer.

Inside, she knew her body was agonizing toward pubescence. This she had studied in school. Outwardly, her body remained stubbornly childlike.

Twelve years gone by since she was born! It felt like an impossible eternity, waiting to pass through childhood, to enter, as if once more, into the world of grown-ups. So she said she was *fourteen* when she could get away with saying so.

Inside, she knew she was somehow older than her physical years. She knew she could see *through* childhood to what was to be beyond it. But that hardly did her any good. Children were treated as children, as if they weren't ever going to grow up. It was all utterly tedious, quite beyond comprehension, being put down if one acted grown-up, and at other times being upbraided for acting childish.

Oakley, her very best friend, wasn't any help. A little plump and tomboyish, Oakley wanted ever so much *never* to grow up -- and she proudly used her child nature to terrorize her parents and teachers who, Oakley often agonized, "have forgotten they ever were children." Sometimes Oakley pouted, too, "Why *does* anyone want to get older? And when they do then spend so much time pretending they're *younger!*"

Alina, of course, didn't have an answer for this bit of wisdom uncharacteristic of Oakley. But sometimes, although she didn't know why, said that "life lived itself over and over again like spring and winter," -- to which Oakley just rolled her eyes around as if all this was just too wearisome and completely unimportant to anything at all.

Oakley loved to race, screeching like a banshee, through the tall corn in summer, over the barren wheat fields in winter. Alina followed, not minding, since Oakley knew better how to be a child than she. This day was no different. Alina, and Oakley, too, raced over the cut wheat fields under the brilliant autumnal sun setting in the western sky, their boots crushing the dried stalks in the dusty furrows. Ahead, at the edge of the field, a dark line of golden yellow cottonwood trees guarded against the strong winds. Only yesterday these trees of gold had been a glaze of summer green against an eternal blue sky. Today they were as a saffron message to Alina from eternity.

Oakley was ahead of Alina, running hard. Alina's uneasy glance backward at her house had slowed her. Alina's mind was lost: Mama didn't think it was ladylike to run races like a boy, but Oakley always teased her into it. Just as quickly as Alina had fallen into this thought, she snapped herself out of her contemplation, assuring herself that wasn't much else to do at the moment anyway. Playing in the house was *out*. No matter how quiet she and Oakley tried to be, one shout or giggle and Mama would be at them about disturbing the Baby, the new Little Richard, born just weeks ago, and on the very day her father has said the View Nam War finally ended.

The cooling wind carried Alina along. Her hair brushed across her cheeks. She could feel the effort of the running, but it almost seemed as if the wind was running for her, making her legs move as it made the tree branches wave about. It was a wind magic, and she and Oakley were being blown along like fallen leaves. Suddenly the song was singing itself to her...

Alina stopped running, stumbling, gripped by inexplicable desolation. A silent memory cry! Lost! Gone! Echoing in her mind.

Alina sank to the ground, her mouth open and tears squeezing past her closed eyelids. Her sudden mourning was mixed with surprise. Lost and found all at once, she looked up. There was Oakley, standing over her, looking triumphant. "What's the matter, Alina? You fall down, you dumb thing!"

"Yes. I was surprised by an old memory," Alina managed to say, trying to giggle through her tears.

"But you are *crying*, you fragile Humpty Dumpty," Oakley said in disgust.

Alina lay back in the plowed furrows, ignoring the teasing. "It's just an old memory. It'll fall back into my heart. They always do."

"You dummy," protested Oakley, plopping down in the dirt next to her. "There's no such thing as an 'old' memory. Isn't a memory just a plain memory?"

"It's a song, silly. An old song that I sort of remember from a long ways back. It's old because it isn't like new memories of learning the state capitals or short division in school. It's something that's already in my heart, and has always been there, and comes from nowhere. So it's got to be an *old* memory, not a new one."

"Honestly, you're so stupid..."

They relaxed in the dirt, watching the late afternoon clouds scudding overhead. "It's a funny memory," Alina continued, "because it's a song and nothing else. It's a song, but it doesn't have any words. It came one evening the other day when I was feeling lost and lonely..."

"Well, *I'm* always feeling lost and lonely," Oakley giggled.

"Not long after Baby came...I sang it to him one night, without even knowing that I knew it. Little Richard quieted down, and pretended he loved it." They could hear the wind rustling the stubble in the field and the humming in the telephone wires along the road. The sound, and the dance of the wind through the trees across the field, stirred something in her. She started humming the wordless song.

"Sounds like just a plain stupid lullaby to me," groaned Oakley, impatient with baby things.

"That's what it is, a lullaby of the winds..."

"You've never been the same since your little baby brother came along," Oakley commented distantly. "And I don't understand why a silly old song makes you cry."

"It's just that it reminds me of...of death...and of life, too."

"Oh! There you go! Always talking about horrid things!"

"Yes, I suppose so. But I don't know what that is. Nobody's died, except grandma, and that was long ago. And everyone stopped crying after the funeral when we all got together at Aunt Margaret's and ate a huge roasted ham and the men drank and smoked, and there was no reason to cry at all."

"Ugh!" Oakley groaned. "Everyone knows your Aunt Margaret is strange when it comes to death and dying, believing all those silly things..."

"Aunt Margaret is *not* strange, but deeply human!" Alina protested firmly. "Besides, you stupid thing yourself, you're making me feel worse instead of better. Who am I to talk to if I can't talk to my best friend? Daddy is impossible, and Mama! Well hardly. Since Baby came, honestly I can't talk to anyone."

"Oh, Alina, you can always talk to me," Oakley groaned with feigned impatience. "After all, it's really just us against our parents. Mine never talk *to* me at all...save to say, 'do this' or 'don't do that'."

"OK," Alina said, jumping up, "but you just quit being so nasty. There, you see! There goes my old memory! It's just blowing away like some stardust across my utterly endless mind." In a blink of any eye she was tearing across the field, far ahead of Oakley, who was screaming "No Fair" far behind.

Finally, of course, they were breathless, lying near a dried-up cow pond, its mud beginning to tighten in the drying winds. The winds were cooling by degrees. Vast storm clouds were gathering in the northeast, but their far-off hue was reflecting golden in the setting sun. In fact, the very air around them had turned saffron colored.

In this golden light, which seemed to abound for eternity, the winds paused to find a new direction in which to blow. Even bubbly Oakley fell into a quiet in the windless silence -- as if not only had the prairie winds stopped, but so had time itself.

"Have you ever thought about time?" Alina finally asked, pensively.

"Oh, there you go again," snorted Oakley, "being...philosophical!"

"I feel like time has no beginning, or ending...it just goes on and on and on."

"How tiresome," Oakley breathed, pretending impatience.

"It's like romance," smiled Alina, deliberately

dragging Oakley into her thoughts, since anything to do with romance had Oakley's immediate attention.

"Ah? How can *that* be?" Oakley demanded.

"Oh, I don't know. I suppose when you are in love, time stops, or something like that."

"That's pretty stupid. How can time stop? It just goes on and on and on."

"Maybe there's no time at all, maybe it's only that we just think there is." Alina's eyes wandered over the darkening horizon, the land now turning mauve and umber beneath a sky now silver grey matching the tone of her own eyes.

"Really, Alina!" chided Oakley with an air of superiority, "you *are* just really bats. You're going to grow up just like your Aunt Margaret!"

"Who says so?" giggled Alina.

"My Mama, that's who says so!" giggled Oakley, "She says you're too *utterly* philosophical for your age."

"And my Mama says you will be a child forever, since you are already a mindless tomboy now." But they both giggled. "Ain't parents utterly boring?" Oakley mused.

But then she continued. "I don't understand anything you say anymore…like when I think of romance, I think of the covers of romance novels down at the supermarket. I certainly don't think of such stupid things like *time* of all things. Novels and romance at least go together."

"Yes, I suppose so…"

"And I'll grow up in my own good time. I'm in no hurry…not even for romance," Oakley spurted out.

The twilight now deepened into a rose red glowing on the western horizon. "Love and time go together," Alina countered, "and they say love never dies."

"Well, who, just *who*, says mush like that?" snorted Oakley.

"The TV, stupid," retorted Alina. "The soaps, always the soaps, you know. Your Mama watches them all the time."

"Oh, those sickening soaps," moaned Oakley. "Who can be bothered with the soaps! My Mama is just a foolish housewife. When I grow up, I'm going to become a racer, and travel around to all the derbies. You just watch me."

Ignoring this, Alina recited: "I wish I could tell you the story of my life." Her eyes grew wide and fixed on the last glowing light in the west, "but it has been bent by too many heavy snows...so many other women have lived...and gone...and travelled in time..."

"Oh, God!" grunted Oakley rising to her feet. "Where, just *where* did you learn that!"

"I read it in a book, a book about an old pixie, like my mother says you are," screamed Alina happily, jumping up, and dashing back through the darkened twilight toward their neighboring homes.

"Oh, Alina, you're positively hopeless," Oakley giggled, whooping passed her.

Chapter
TWO

R ichard had been born into sturdy Nebraskan farm folk, who generations back had first broken the prairie sod and made it grow not grass but sorghum and wheat and maize and, here and there, fields of tall standing corn. His father had claimed that his blood ran thick with the love of the earth, and that his heart beat in time with the farm's four seasons of planting, growing, harvesting and then selling what was harvested.

Despite this, and perhaps even because of it, Richard had been marched off to college and had ended up an attorney who specialized in adjudicating land claims. A good thing for him, too, for now the small town nearby was growing outward, expanding as a result of the nonstop subdividing of the farms that had once only been endless reaches of grass bowing this way and that to the whim of the prairie winds.

Although Richard had not the nuances of the fertile earth or the seasons in him, he did have the logic and intricacies of law and legal foul-ups. But then many said that lawyers didn't have hearts at all, that having one, that is a heart, was bad for a lawyer's business. Yet Richard's veins were filled with same farm blood that had run in his family stretching back to the first ones who had come west and he was content to live not in the growing outward town, but in the old, big farmhouse of his father, and his father's father and those even further back, and this pleased Julia, too. This home, which had been in his family for as far back on the family tree Richard could trace, was all that Richard knew and it had been filled with love despite whatever hardships its inhabitants had endured.

These days, however, his peace abiding home was not very peaceful at all. Julia was stressed out with all that entailed with tending to Little Richard. Neither of them had been prepared for this new family addition, a little one who had come along to them, unexpectedly, nearly thirteen years after Alina had grasped onto her life.

Not wanting another child after nearly losing their Alina, Julia was often heard saying: "I can't bear going through that again."

But then one day, there was squalling Little Richard, and that was that -- except that Julia was, now nearly thirteen years later, somewhat out of sorts with tending a crying infant babe.

Alina had never *squalled* -- at least not very much. She had grown independently and calmly, as if she had known how to do so. Strangely, perhaps even eerily, Alina, as time went on, had seemed to know how to do everything, including cooking supper now that Little Richard was stressing Julia so much.

Richard, who was used to having things go along without much interrupting, took it for granted and didn't think much upon it. All this fitted well into his lawyer's logical heart and mind.

So it was that after her caper with Oakley, Alina had cooked supper. Against the rising night wind, the house was warm and soft inside -- except that the wonderful old house was now filled with a mixture of unaccustomed noise.

"Honestly," grumbled Richard, coming out from behind his evening paper to fumble over his pipe, "can't you turn the TV down, Alina. Between it and Little Richard and the wind outside, well the noise level..."

"No problem, Daddy," agreed Alina. "There's nothing worthy on it tonight, anyway."

"Really, Alina. Don't be so snooty."

Alina sighed and rolled her eyes. "Little Richard *is* crying *too* much."

"Just like you, when you were little," mused Richard smiling to himself as he retreated behind his paper once more.

"He's just scared of the wind..." began Alina.

"Ah, hum..."

"And, we're going to have an early snow, too."

"Ah, hum..."

"And Santa Claus came and told me an obscene tale out by the cow pond today..."

"Hum..."

Alina rolled her eyes, and shrugged, and turned the TV down a little. It was going to snow for sure, since the TV had said so. Up at Lincoln it was already freezing. It was odd how a fifty-mile distance could make a big difference in Nebraskan weather patterns.

"Well, I hope it snows, anyway," Alina mused to herself. There were the dishes to do. Mama simply would be too tired. There was a Star Trek rerun to watch while doing dish duty. "Honestly, Daddy could read the papers for the most endless time," she almost said out loud but caught herself. She looked over at him as he emerged again and left wordlessly for his study in which he could spend such unending time, too.

The wind was building up outside, shivering across the open fields, undaunted by the aged windbreak poplars that lined fields and roads everywhere, and whose yellow leaves were blowing off. Aunt Margaret always said that the sodbusters should have planted pines, which didn't lose their needles against the winter winds. The house was under a weather attack, the winds hitting the sides, causing long sighs and wails and creakings.

Alina was content, though, her hands in Ivory Liquid, her mind in the far reaches of outer space, her attention drawn every now and then to Little Richard whose wails grew worse and worse upstairs. Finally, she was upstairs herself, bathing, getting ready for bed.

"For Chrissakes, Julia," Richard shouted from downstairs, "can't you get the boy quieted down?"

"It was going to be one of *those* nights," sighed Alina to herself, "since Daddy had used one of those words."

"Richard," Julia sternly called back down the stairs, "if his crying bothers you, close your study door. I don't know what's wrong with him."

"Yes," acknowledged Alina to herself, snuggling deeper into her warm nightgown, "it was definitely one of *those* nights. Mama never spoke *sternly* except when she was in one of her stressed-out moods and about to get really angry."

Alina finished washing herself around her ears with one of the fancy red washcloths *nobody* was supposed to use except company. She was warm and clean. She looked closely in the mirror to see if somehow the hot tears of the afternoon had left any traces. Nothing there. Baby was really crying. It was definitely the frightening winds whose cold fingers were trying to invade the house. Well, she would have to do something about that. After all, men weren't very brave while they were still babies, and that she knew for sure, and the strong winds sounded like bombs going off, sometimes.

She went into Little Richard's room. She found her mother trying to sing him lullabies, but he was squalling anyway. "I swear, I don't know what's the matter," Julia said tiredly. "Perhaps I should call up Doc Thompson. Perhaps he wouldn't mind coming over. He should have finished supper by now."

"He's just scared of the wind," Alina said with a soft conviction. "I'll sing him a windy song, and then he won't mind it."

"What's a windy song?" Julia asked, bothered with suggestions as usual. "Something you learned at school?"

"No, not at school," Alina murmured. She took one of Little Richard's flailing hands and softly sang the wordless melody that welled up from her heart. The melody sounded like a wind, too, but it came not from the elements outside that could be so cruel, but from a human love and compassion. With that, the delicate melody of the windy song joined with the noisy rage of the elements buffeting the house outside, and Little Richard looked around wildly for the source of this new, comforting sound. When his little eyes found Alina's, he began burping, even though he was lying down. In a few moments he had stopped crying, and then smiled as best he might.

The sensations of old memories of the windy song again came alive within Alina. Her heart expanded somehow, seeming to mature. A mother's love poured through her soft song, from her to the baby boy -- but this time the memory of the windy song brought comfort, not fear or tears.

Little Richard smiled, his fat cheeks red and wet. He burped again, and managed to struggle a little in his warm wrappings, looking braver already in his new world of Pampers and baby-blue blankets.

As Alina looked down at him, the space between them seemed to shrink. A young man, her heart knew, who was scared of the windy noise and needed lots of love. Soon his eyelids were drooping. Alina felt something inside her say, "now he knows he needn't be scared at all."

He went to sleep.

Silently, Alina helped her mother tuck the blankets over the sleeping infant, careful not to make any sounds at all. They walked together back to her room and once there, Alina was being tucked in herself.

"Mama," she said after Julia had listened to the usual prayer, "when can I start staying up like Oakley does? She stays up until ten."

"Maybe next spring," Julia said, "but a lot of sleep will help keep those old colds and flu away through the winter."

"Yes, I suppose so," Alina said begrudgingly.

Julia bent down to kiss her goodnight. "That was a nice song, a nice melody, Alina. Where did you learn it?"

"I didn't learn it, I merembered it."

"The word is 'remembered'," Julia said, grinning.

"I know," Alina replied, "but I like 'merember' better."

"Well, all right, but just this once," Julia

laughed. "But where do you *merember* the song from?"

"Oh, when I had babies, too, I guess."

"You mean the babies in your doll house?"

"No. *Real* babies. Just like Little Richard. I sang them that song when the wind was blowing." As she thought of the windy song, sleep began to waft over her. She smiled, mostly to herself, then to her mother. She was too sleepy to notice that Julia had gotten noticeably quiet.

"Alina, dear," Julia asked slowly, "when was it that you had real babies just like your father and me?"

"Oh, Mama, don't you know? It was before I died."

The warm cloud of sleep came down over her, escorted by the wind and the old song another mother at another time had taught her.

Julia looked down at her daughter and didn't know what to think or do.

Chapter
THREE

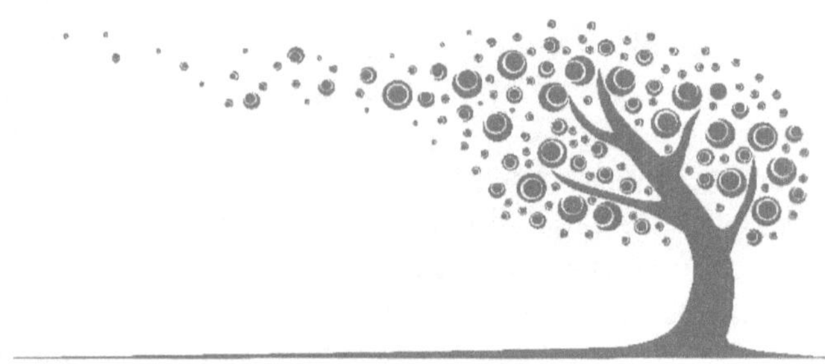

Julia found herself lingering silently beside her sleeping daughter, feeling lost in a sudden, incomprehensible moment, laced with her tiredness and...a sudden surge of fear.

Her auburn hair fell loose over her shoulders, her face pale, well-formed, like her daughter's. She thought briefly that Alina could easily grow up to be the town beauty, as she herself had once been. Alina's strange words had made her feel older. Julia's shoulder's sagged, her features softened by the pink light filtering through the bedside lamp whose base was a smiling panda bear. She couldn't help but wish it was the wind that had said those last few words and not her child. Her frown deepened. She realized she was just sitting there, half paralyzed by the simple majesty of "Oh, Mama, don't you know. It was before I died..."

The incomprehensible moment forming inside her now grew until it seemed it was a vast dark space opening up somewhere, she knew not where, to an inexplicable place inside her everyday thinking mind. Through her confusion she turned off the panda-bear lamp, and found herself somehow in the hall at the top of the stairs. There she held onto the banister for a few moments until the lump in her throat dissolved.

Richard was sitting in his study, puffing his pipe in his usual calm way. She frowned again, sniffing. The aromatic smoke pleased her sometimes, offended at others. She surveyed Richard, pausing in the doorway.

The irony of middle age that was suiting Richard, was decaying her own looks. He had grown a little gaunt around the jaw, the neck, but his hair was still young, as were his eyes and hands. She was content to have married him after the glorious beauty-queen days -- when there was nothing left to do except try to marry well.

"Really, Richard," she began. "I *do* resent being yelled at when I'm having troubles with the baby."

Richard continued to puff; his attention fixed into the piles of papers on his desk. Julia felt a betraying quiver in her threat, and the tears and sobbing came before she could make an effort to stop them. She collapsed into a wing-backed chair, holding its padded arms tightly.

At this, Richard came out of his papers and smoke cloud. "Ah, Julia, this is really nothing to cry about. I'm sorry I yelled up at you. Had a somewhat rough day, you know."

At this, Julia only cried harder. Richard came and put his arms around her shoulders.

"Oh, Rich, it wasn't the yelling. Alina just scared me to death, I suppose."

Richard raised his eyebrows. Julia's usual confrontations with their daughter occasioned irritation, not fear.

"Something she said," Julia continued, "something strange and frightening."

"But what was it?" Richard's strong hands pulled her shaking body to him. The familiar and comforting aromas of his body and nearness embraced her with more force than his arms could. Julia felt herself relax.

"Well, she sang a song to Little Richard. There weren't any words to it, just a melody, but it was lovely, and it put him right to sleep."

"About time, too," Richard said. "What's so bad about that?"

"I'd never heard her sing it before, and I asked her if she'd learned it at school or something." Julia's words tightened, "and she said...it was just when she was dropping off herself...that it was from...*before she died*!"

Pressed against Richard's chest, she was prepared for the note of forced patience in his voice. "You sure you heard that right, Julia? When you go to sleep, you say funny things sometimes, it's like your mind goes out of gear, or you're already halfway into a dream."

"It *wasn't* like that, Rich! It was so...so *certain*, so matter of fact. And when she was singing, well...she suddenly seemed *too* grown-up."

"Merciful God Almighty, Julia!" Richard's grip was almost painful on her upper arms as he held her out from him and looked at her with a tight face. "Do you see those papers over there? I've been going through them all day to see if I can find a way not to call in Frank Pierce's loan, and now you're coming to me with some crazy stuff about Alina dying before she was born? I swear, I don't know why you can't handle your own daughter without collapsing..."

"Richard," she said hotly, "you can't yell it away. I saw Alina when she was singing to the baby, and I heard what she said later. I know she meant what she said. I know it's all too impossible, Rich, but she seemed so certain. I could actually

...believe that it was a mother who sang Little Richard that, song."

Outside the house, the windy gale had increased, pummeling the home from the north. Richard found himself frowning. He shrugged, drawing her closer into his arms.

"Now, Julia, children have all sorts of fantasies. You know that. Let's don't let this thing become too real. After all, you know very well that such things aren't possible!"

"I just said *that*, Richard!" But Julia was collecting herself, seeking a tissue for her nose. Richard reached for his flagging pipe. The aromatic smoke curled once more into the winterish feeling invading the rooms.

"But, it's all so...so morbid," muttered Julia, suppressing a new volume of tears.

"Well," Richard mused, happy that this scene appeared to be drawing to an end, "I suppose children think about death just as adults do, only they probably imagine all sorts of things." He resumed his chair, preparing to become absorbed into his evening's work.

A hot flash of new irritation crossed Julia's face. "Richard, children don't think about death...at least not with the conviction Alina just had."

"All right! All right, Julia! What do you want me to do about it? I think we ought to leave her alone. She'll forget about it...whatever *it* was."

"I don't know what I want you to do. I've heard her humming that...that windy song to herself for a few days now. I fully believe she associates it with a morbid idea of some sort, or at least possibly so. Perhaps we ought to have her see Doctor Thompson?"

"Why? Whatever for? Children are sometimes quite wild in their fantasies, but they always pass."

"Richard, this isn't a fantasy. After all, I did see her sing to Baby, and see that it had a strange effect on him."

"Okay! Okay," said Richard, raising his hands and giving in. "I'll talk to her in the morning...and then you'll soon see it's nothing much at all."

"Oh, Richard, would you? I'm sure you can reason with her. You're particularly good at that."

Chapter
FOUR

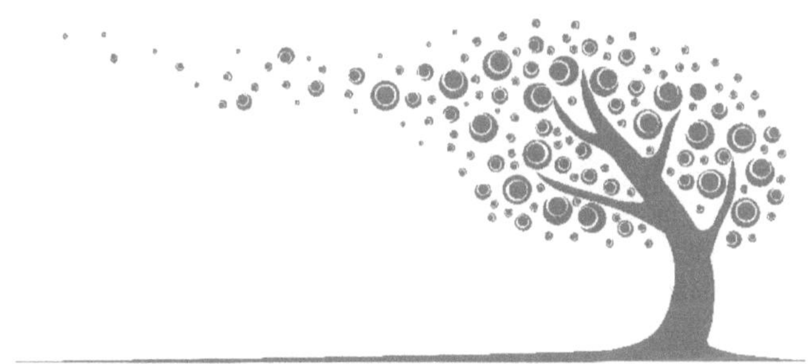

Mornings were always best in the house, especially cold mornings. Coffee smells mixed with the clatter of Mama making pancakes or French toast, floated up the stairs. Outside both the wind and the temperature had dropped.

Alina stood before the mirror affixed to the back of her bedroom door, looking at her reflection. She was dressed, she could see that! But...she somehow looked different from the way she had yesterday. Was it that she was a day older?

A furrow creased her forehead as a small thought crossed her inner awareness. She couldn't quite grab it. It flitted too fast -- quick like the small and beautiful hummingbirds that sometimes passed through Nebraska on their way to somewhere else. Yes, it was a thought like *that*, gone before you could see what it was.

She glanced out the window. Today was Saturday, and it would be an indoors day. Mama would probably say it was too cold to go outside. Alina sighed. She hardly ever had one of those colds Mama was worried she'd get.

Daddy looked directly at her when she came

into the breakfast alcove just off the kitchen. She was surprised. Saturday was Daddy's half-day at the office. He usually left for work earlier. "Silly Daddy are you sick or something?" she asked in a mock professional manner, kissing him on the cheek.

"Nope," Richard said, forcing a grin. "I just thought I'd drive to the office a little later this morning."

Alina quickly drank a glass of cold milk waiting at her place on the table. Julia brought in a stack of steaming hot pancakes, threw Richard a significant look, and retreated into the kitchen.

"Mama says you sang a new song to Little Richard last night," Richard began.

"Oh, yes Daddy! The windy song," Alina said through a mouthful of pancake and syrup. She looked around for Julia, who usually scolded if she spoke with her mouth filled.

"The windy song?"

"Yes, that's what it's called."

Richard took a deep breath. "You frightened your Mama, you know, when you talked about it. Did you learn…uh, the windy song at school or some place?"

"No, not at school…" Alina sat back in her chair and looked directly at him. The new posture suddenly confused Richard, although he didn't know why. It seemed that she was taller, somehow more…he hunted silently for the word…more competent, in a strange way.

"Well, where, then, did you learn it?" he continued.

"Once, a long time ago…when I had real babies. I sang it to them…then."

A look of some kind that Richard couldn't explain seemed to appear in Alina's face. "But

Alina, surely you mean your dolls or…"

"No, Daddy. Real babies, just like Little Richard, only they had different names. The oldest was…Jimmy J, and the other…was David."

Richard was now silent for a moment, confused, disturbed inside his logical self. The strength of Alina's emotion caused his eyes to widen. His hand fluttered, then sought for his pipe, plunging into a secure pocket. A tinge of fear touched his senses. He cleared his throat.

"Alina, sometimes…well, sometimes children, grownups, too, of course, well, people of all ages, sometimes think some strange things, and these things, well, they're just imagination or something like that."

"No, Daddy, this isn't imagin-a-tion. Oakley and I play imagin-a-tion games all the time. They're fun, like when we used to imagine our mud pies were really pies, and we put rocks in them and imagined that the rocks were chocolate chips or apricots or something else."

"I see, then," said Richard, not quite keeping the irritation out of his voice. "What would you say these…uh, these *real* babies are, then?"

"Why, *real* babies, of course, only they must be almost grown up by now," said Alina cheerfully.

"What do you mean 'grown up'?"

"Well, that was a long time ago…before this time now," responded Alina. "Yes! That *was* it," she said silently to herself. *That* was the small thought. She caught it, bringing it more into remembering. A flush of hot concern suddenly lit her face rosy pink.

"Why Alina," asked Richard, "what's wrong? Are you sick?"

"No, Daddy…not sick. It's just that…" she paused.

"Just what, Alina, darling?" asked Richard, reaching toward her. Something in her voice brought up a surge of tenderness.

"It's just...I was wondering how they are," mused Alina, "*where* they are by now."

Richard caught himself just before his fingers touched her arm.

"My two sons..."

Richard was surprised as he began to shake. Hot rage poured up his spine. It came up and caught in his throat, where it rested like a solid scalding lump. Why should he feel rage, he wondered, trying desperately to control it before it controlled him. He had almost risen from his chair to slap his daughter.

Thankfully, her next words cut through his hot anger like the cold winds outside. "Daddy, can you take me to see them? I wonder how they are...that is, I wonder if they're being cared for as they should have been." She now looked at Richard with a direct earnestness.

Standing in the alcove doorway, listening in to this conversation, Julia gasped and her face blanched. "Richard," began Julia with a small wail.

"Don't interrupt us!" said Richard thickly. His eyes narrowed at his daughter. "Where are they, Alina, where are these two...uh, sons of..." He couldn't finish.

Alina's forehead wrinkled in thought.

"Richard, really!" Julia protested.

"Be quiet!" Richard snapped.

"Daddy, they're up at Lincoln," Alina stated with utmost calmness.

"Richard, really..." Julia interrupted again, her lips trembling.

"Julia! Please let Alina and I talk this out. What

about Lincoln, Alina?"

"Well, that's where they are, in Lincoln, Nebraska," Alina said, but with an important tone of discovery deepening her voice.

"*Who* is she *talking* about, Richard?" asked Julia, her voice shrill.

"Oh, Mama, my two babies, only they must be bigger now."

The two parents looked at her in shocked silence. Julia gave a broken sob and ran back into the kitchen.

"What's the matter with Mama, Daddy?" asked Alina.

Richard cleared his throat. "What you've been saying has scared your mother a little," he said, forcing calmness into his voice.

"Oh, gosh, she shouldn't get scared."

"I don't think she would get scared if she could be convinced that you're dreaming or imagining these...things. After all, you are old enough now to realize that such strange things scare people. Why, soon you'll be a young lady."

"Yes, I know all that, Daddy. But this is really real, too. I merember them, and they...the memories are..."

"'Remember', Alina, the words *remember*," Richard said, another chill wave going through him.

"Yes," agreed Alina, the faraway look returning to her face. "Yes, I know, but I *do* remember them. They both looked like their father."

There was a sound of commotion from the kitchen, then Oakley, bundled against the cold, ran into the breakfast room. Richard ignored her.

"Their father?" he said slowly.

"Why yes, Daddy, you don't think I could have

real babies without a father for them, do you?" "Alina!" screeched Oakley, "let's go out and run around. You can see your breath in the air, and there's frost under the trees!"

"Oh, Daddy, *can* I?" begged Alina, reaching for her wraps. Under his dismay Richard felt a brief stir of amusement. He knew, as well as Alina, that Julia, if consulted, would insist they play in the rumpus room in the basement.

"Yes, of course," he said. He had come to a decision, and it would be best to talk to Julia about it with no chance of interruption. "Only, don't go too far. Your Mama is…uh, taking you to see Doc Thompson this afternoon."

"Okay, Daddy." The door slammed behind the two girls.

Richard sat there lost in thought. A huge weight descended on him as words raced through his mind: "How, and in this strangest of ways, did their daughter, for twelve, years, thirteen now almost, so perfectly normal and usual and dependable, slip away from them and the intimate familiarity within which he had known her? But more so, this had happened so suddenly and without any warning, and in such a way that neither he nor Julia knew what to do or say or think. For never in their lives had either of them had even the merest idea that their daughter might ever say to them what she had."

CONFUSIONS

"That is the land of lost content,
I see it shining plain,
The happy highways where I went
And cannot come again."

— A. E. Housman
Poem XL, A Shropshire Lad
1896

Chapter
FIVE

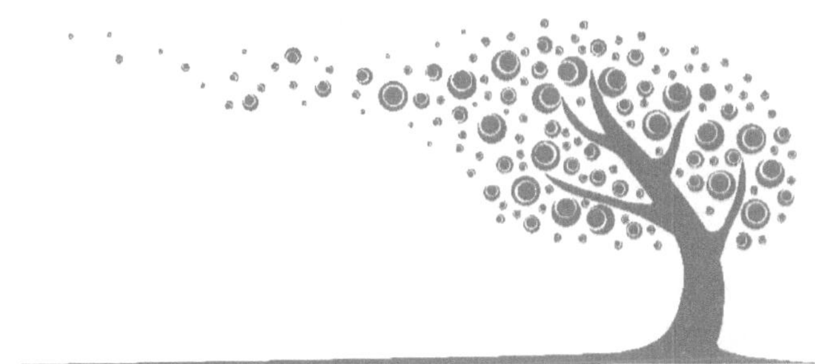

After Alina and Oakley had scampered into the cold autumn air outside, Richard regained himself and went to find Julia upstairs in the bedroom lying silently on the bed. He sat down beside her and began to rub her hand. "All right, Richard," she said tonelessly. "You heard her…saw her. What are you going to do?"

Her hand was cold and unresponsive as he rubbed it. "Well," he said uneasily, "I don't know if it's all that serious. Perhaps she'll forget…"

"Richard!" Julia pulled her hand away and propped herself up on one elbow.

Richard continued. "Look, she seemed…all right, happy as ever when she ran outside with Oakley."

"You didn't let her go *outside* in this cold? She'll come down with something."

Richard relaxed at this. For once, Julia's fussing about Alina's activity came as a welcome relief. "I think you're too concerned about that," he said. "If she gets sick, she gets sick. But we can't make her behave differently from other kids, and all of 'em are out playing today. First real winter day, you know. No snow yet. But winterish, anyway."

"Oh, stop trying to pretend all this is normal. She'll be going on thirteen shortly, and she's kind of acting like that, then she acts like she was four or five years younger, then she acts as if she was someone else...What did she say to you after I ran back into the kitchen?"

"She said something about the...babies. That you had to have a father to make real babies. Then noisy Oakley came in and I let her go."

Julia closed her eyes. "*What* are we going to *do*, Rich? I can't stand this...*change* in her. Don't pretend it isn't there, either! Can't you see how *certain* she is about all this? Believe me! I know her too well. She isn't pretending. She has *never* pretended. This isn't going to go away."

Richard sighed again. Yes, in a blinding moment, he had indeed seen something about Alina that he'd never seen before. He didn't know what it was, exactly, but whatever it was it now took away the faint hope that his daughter had been indulging in some childish game.

"No, I can't think that, now," he agreed slowly. "I can't claim to know what to do about it, either. You'd best call up Doc Thompson and take Alina down to him. I already told her you'd be seeing him this afternoon. He's known her inside and out since she was born, and if anyone can figure what this is all about and what to do about it, he can. Now I'd better get over to the office, or I'll have to face a lot of jokes about keeping lawyers' hours."

Julia looked at him with a brief smile, then closed her eyes again. Tears came from beneath the shut lids. "It scares me so much," she said in a muffled voice. "Alina...talking about dying...then talking about the *sex thing*!"

"The *what*?"

"Making babies! Why should she be thinking

about such things now. Why, she's only twelve, and still a child..."

Richard considered this dubiously. "Oh, for Chrissakes, Julia, kids her age think about stuff like that. But I kind of doubt she's got any clear idea of what she's talking about," he said. "Listen, you leave all that up to Doc Thompson to find out."

"I wonder if she's been spending too much time with Margaret," Julia said. Richard sighed yet again and looked at his wristwatch. Julia stood up and started smoothing the bed. "Margaret talks about such odd things as if they're real...the occult and trash like that. I'd hate to think it runs somewhere in the family, *your* family." She let drop the sheet she was pulling taut as Richard reached out and hugged her.

"Alina'll be all right," he murmured in her ear. "You just call ahead to Doc Thompson and give him an idea of what's bothering us. He'll know what to do about it right off. So you leave it up to him, huh? Richard's attention shifted just then, "Hey, what's wrong with Little Richard? Haven't heard a yell out of him this morning."

"Well, he *has* been good...ever since Alina started singing that melody to him. You know, he tried to say a word, I think, when I fed him."

"Great! What word?"

"Well, it may have been food, or good...I don't really know."

"Say, I'd better look in on the young fellow, see if we can start up a man-to-man talk." He released her and started toward the bedroom door.

"Rich?"

He stopped.

"You know, that's the first time in weeks..."

"First time?"

"That you've gone to see him before you went

to work."

Richard paused and looked quizzically at his wife. "That's...well, maybe it is, maybe it is, Julia."

He left the room and stopped, putting his head back through the doorway. "You'll call me after you get back from Thompson's, okay? I'll want to hear all about what he had to say. Listen, don't worry, Doc'll get her away from all that nonsense!"

Chapter
SIX

In the brittle but fresh outside, the morning sun was riding high already. Beneath the cold touch of the northern prairie winds, hoar frost had festooned everything, although it was largely melted by now. The earth itself had seemed to recede, and in its place the sky overhead to grow. It was almost a new world, denuded of green and leaves and warmth.

"Race you across the field," screamed Oakley, taking a quick head start as usual.

"My Mama says you're an utter tomboy," screeched Alina in hot pursuit. "An' my Mama says your Mama treats you like a delicate doll," taunted Oakley in return.

The girls reached the far end of the field, both giggling and out of breath. The ground was now solidly frozen, and they had been able to dash swiftly, two winter-wrapped nymphs in a magical, if melting, landscape. Their frosty breaths spurted out into the air in front of them. The cow pond gleamed a bit of blue ice.

"Oh, I do like going fast," exclaimed Alina, her eyes sparkling, cold water droplets of excitement clinging to their corners.

"ZZZooom...Oh, so do I!" groaned Oakley. "I'll

be glad when I'm old enough to drive a car. I'm going to be a professional racer, and then I can drive about a thousand miles an hour!"

"Okay, yes," Alina responded vaguely as a dark shadow passed through her eyes. She looked up to see if it was a cloud crossing the sun despite the sky being cold-blue and clear.

"What's the matter, now?" Oakley snorted, squatting on the frozen mud, skimming a rock across the thin ice.

"Now? Nothing...it was just a dark thought..."

"Oh! You're simply impossible, always having strange thoughts." But Oakley's curiosity was aroused as usual. "What kind of a thought?"

"Oh, I don't know really. Kind of a speeding thought...like driving very fast. Only it was a long time ago. Before I was born to this time now."

"Puleeze, just *please* don't go and get philosophical again..." But at this, the bubbly tomboy, Oakley, herself suddenly broke into tears. "You scare me with such stupid ideas! Soon your Dad'll drag you off to a therapy or something! And everyone will blame your crazy aunt."

At this, Alina grinned and stood up. "Yes!" she said, smiling, "That's it, I've got to go and ask Aunt Margaret."

"Oh, such garbage!" groaned Oakley. "Don't say it was *my* idea."

Chapter
SEVEN

Alina loved everything about her Aunt Margaret. In a way, her aunt was an older copy of her mother, but not really. They had the same stature, though, and both had been local beauty queens. Whereas her mother was cool and detached, her aunt was buxom and warm and involved. She wore her greying auburn hair piled on her head, old-fashioned, matronly. Her mother, trying to stay young, usually wore hair loose so that it flowed over her shoulders.

Aunt Margaret's spirit reached out, enfolding everyone. Alina could see that her mother didn't understand that soft, popular nature. Maybe that was why her mother was distant, not wanting to be too much like her father's older sister. If both, each in their own time, had once been the town beauty, Aunt Margaret had always been the most loved and popular, and so perhaps her mother resented this a little, even though she had been voted beautiful herself.

Nevertheless, it was true that her aunt cried awfully easily, and went on about strange things, even talking with the spirits of those gone.

But if this irritated her mother, which it usually did, it only increased her aunt's ambience in a farming community where old people were always dying and wakes were always going on.

She lived in her own old, large farmhouse that had been in *her* husband's family for five generations. It was filled with old things, hardly anything modern at all, except, of course, the plumbing and electricity. There were old fireplaces and crystal chandeliers, and some of the windows had stained glass through which the sun cast lovely ruby and sapphire patterns over worn oriental carpets. The heavy furniture was *very* worn. Aunt Margaret never threw away anything, and seemed not to like new things at all.

It was in this house that she lived alone, ever since Uncle Ned had been crushed under a hay baler somewhere out in the fields. Aunt Margaret now owned those fields, too, and although they were overgrown with weeds, land developers continually offered to buy them for a shopping mall or something else. Alina had heard in the normal way that children hear everything – by listening -- that her father and Aunt Margaret had terrific arguments over that, since he thought it would be a good idea to sell the farm and invest the money so that Aunt Margaret could have a larger income.

Even though Aunt Margaret would give in almost any time anyone wanted her to do something, when it came to old things, she dug in her heels and wouldn't budge. After all, the farm was an old thing and had been in Uncle Ned's family for generations. Alina loved her aunt all the more, because she herself loved old things, too.

Aunt Margaret's house was always filled with delicious smells; she was always preserving or roasting or baking something. Today was no exception and the house was filled with the scent of apples stewing for sauce. Alina barged right into the kitchen where two huge pots were bubbling away on the stove as Aunt Margaret was steaming Bell jars and lids.

"All the apples in the root cellar were starting to turn a little," Aunt Margaret said cheerfully. "So I thought I'd put them up. Apple sauce is ever so good on cold winter mornings and evenings, too, don't you think, Alina? Plus I promised that new young Reverend Matthews I'd give him some as soon as it's finished. He seems so lost, so alone here, poor thing. He belongs in a big city."

"Daddy says he's a soft revolutionary," muttered Alina, "whatever *that* means."

"Well, your father doesn't know everything. Reverend Matthews can't be an exact replica of mean old Reverend Andrews, you know, may his soul rest in peace."

"True," Alina agreed sagely. "I think he's sexy."

Aunt Margaret smiled in mock astonishment. "Sometimes, Alina dear, I don't know if you're growing up too fast."

Alina flung her coat onto a chair, sampled the spicy sauce with a wooden spoon, and set to helping her aunt with steaming the jars.

But Aunt Margaret did all the work faster, and so Alina just mostly hung around, keeping company. Aunt Margaret had one other attribute that endeared her to Alina: she was the only grown-up person that she could talk with about deep things -- and it surely was a deep thing she wanted to talk about right now!

So she sat down at the large oval kitchen table, and plunged her chin into her cupped hands. "Aunt Margaret, do people live before?"

"Before what, honey?"

"You know. Before they're born."

Aunt Margaret stopped her chore of filling jars and looked quietly at her niece. "You know, I promised your parents not to talk about such things with you, or even in front of you."

"Oh, how stupid," Alina snorted. She could see Aunt Margaret's lips beginning to quiver. "Mama and Daddy never talk about anything at *all*," she continued, "except the weather, Little Richard, the Daddy's job, and what's for supper and what's on TV...and who comes into the Daddy's office...and their stupid bridge club. How am I supposed to learn *anything*?" Alina was suddenly angry and broke into tears.

"Why, Alina, honey. Whatever is the matter?" Aunt Margaret folded Alina into her arms, pressing her against her full chest.

"Oh, Aunt Margaret! It's all so *awful*. I can *remember* something. At least I think it's a memory, and not an imagination. It's so real."

"Hush, now, and stop those tears. You know, my dear, what's real to some people is often not very real to others, and there are some things it's better not to talk about at all."

"Yes, I know *that*!" Alina agreed, but sourly. "Like your spirits, and all those psychic books you read."

"Well, my realities are different, and I do know that some other people will laugh at them. But I'm too old to care about what other people think. One day I'll join my Ned. He's here in the house waiting for me. That's a great comfort for me. He was all I ever wanted in life, and I know that we'll meet again. But you're too young to...well, it's best for you to grow up normal like everyone else."

"But that's stupid, Aunt Margaret. I asked my teachers what normal was and I still haven't found *that* out."

"People will become very unkind if you talk about these other things as though you mean them."

"I do mean it, Aunt Margaret. I *can* remember something." Aunt Margaret paused, studying Alina for a silent moment.

"Then forget those memories," she said quietly. "I'm warning you, Alina, people will be unkind."

"Aunt Margaret!" Alina gasped. "*You* can remember something, too, can't you?"

Aunt Margaret lowered her head, breathing deeply. "That was a long time ago, dear child, so very long ago."

"But what happened?" Alina demanded in awe; her eyes wide.

Now, seeing something profoundly serious in her niece, Aunt Margaret stopped fussing with jars and lids and sauce and sat down, smoothed her apron, and then looked into her own memories. "It was so exceptionally beautiful at first: I could remember dying peacefully at a ripe old age, dying in bed, properly, you know, and with my family all round me. I could remember that so very well. It seemed like such a good full life. That was why I never minded funerals, since it seemed to me that there was…well, you know, that dying was a transition of some sort."

The worn soul that was now called Margaret gazed into a past long lost, long gone. "Then, once when we were quite young, your father and me, your grandmother took us to a funeral. I didn't act very sad, and so your grandmother asked me about it, why I wasn't crying like Richard."

She went on: "We were supposed to cry at funerals, you know."

Aunt Margaret's eyes seemed to be seeing invisible things, and her voice had turned dreamy.

Alina was fascinated. "Yes, Aunt Margaret, what happened?"

"Well, I told my mama…about dying, and that I could *remember*…" Aunt Margaret stopped and tears spilled onto her cheeks.

"C'mon, Aunt Margaret," Alina scolded. "It's stupid to cry. What *happened*?"

"Your grandmother took me to the minister, and, oh my, did he just whoop and howl and rage that the devil was in me!" The tears drying on her cheeks, Aunt Margaret gave a brief, wry smile. "Your grandmother locked me in the upstairs bedroom until I stopped talking about it. Everyone prayed for me. Pretty soon everybody forgot about it."

Almost as though reeling from the experience now decades later she went on, "Years later your Uncle Ned and I talked about things like that, but just between ourselves. It's safer to…Oh! Look at the sauce! It's getting finished!" She took the large pots off the stove. "So you see, honey, it's best not to talk about such memories. There are a lot of things that life makes you keep to yourself."

Alina said slowly, with admiration, "Aunt Margaret, isn't it a shame to have to…to push *away* that you remember something like that?"

"It is, my dear," Aunt Margaret said gravely. "Well, it probably is. It's like…making it so you don't see or hear as well as you really could. But that's the way people are, you have to be. For Heaven's sake, don't tell anything like this to your parents! Your mother would just about have a fit!"

Alina laughed. "I think they're both already having fits."

"Alina!" Aunt Margaret rolled her eyes upward. "Do you mean you've *already* started something?"

"I couldn't help it, Aunt Margaret! All of a sudden I was singing a song I never heard, then I just started remembering things..."

Aunt Margaret's lips were quivering again. "Oh, Alina, dear, you just try to forget all about that. Whatever those memories are, they represent past things. You have to live for the future. That's the important thing, only the future."

"It's true," Alina murmured softly. "The past *is* gone! There's only the future to live for. I guess you're right, Aunt Margaret."

Aunt Margaret gave a sigh of relief, and smiled a little, wiping the corners of her eyes. "Oh, look at all the sauce now. It's getting too thick to pour."

"I have to go, Aunt Margaret," Alina said. "Daddy says I have to have a checkup at the doctor's office this afternoon."

Aunt Margaret turned away from the stove. "You had a checkup at the beginning of summer, didn't you?"

"Sure. Just after school got out."

"Huh. And now another one...Tell me, dear, did you just now find out about this checkup?"

"Yup. Daddy told me this morning, just after I gave him a fit."

"Well." Aunt Margaret narrowed her eyes. "You say hellow to old Doc Thompson for me, won't you, Alina? He's a fine man, always was. And don't you go worrying your mama and daddy with old memories that don't belong."

Chapter
EIGHT

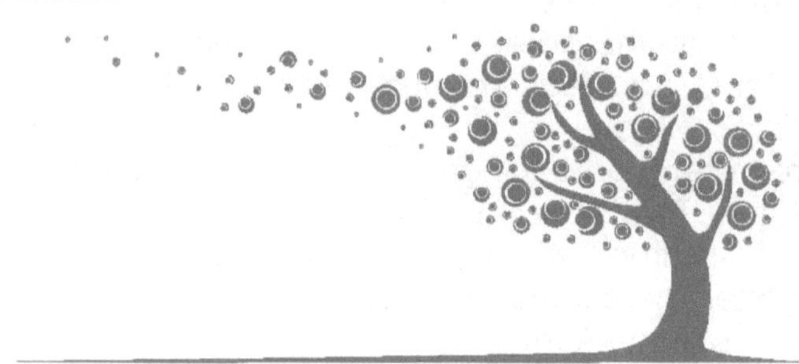

Julia deposited Alina in a chair and went over to the nurse, old Miss Hautman. Alina heard some urgent whispering, then Mama went into the inner office and closed the door. The waiting room was filled as usual. Alina sort of loved it, somehow. People were always gossiping, always comparing notes on tidbits that made up life: pregnancies, miscarriages, who had cancer, who had arthritis, lumbago, who was to not gonna make it, who was to succeed in living, all those things that disgusted Oakley, but sort of fascinated her. Today, though, no one was saying much.

After a while, her mother came out, looking worried and angry. "Doc'll be ready for you in a minute," she said tersely. But Alina smiled, for she loved Doc Thompson. Most people did. They said he was as up to date as any physician in Lincoln or Omaha, but still kept his warm, old-fashioned manner and country ways. His bright blue eyes and bush brows always made Alina laugh inside herself. She thought he looked more like a big elf than a doctor.

A sharp buzz came from old Miss Hautman's desk. The nurse listened, then looked over to her.

"Doctor will see you now, Alina."

"All right, my little beauty," Doc said, "take a deep breath while I listen to see if you still have some lungs."

Alina laughed. *"Of course* I do, silly doctor." But she breathed deeply, anyhow.

"OK, that was fine, now once more." Alina held her breath this time. "Aha!" snorted Doc Thompson, "just as I thought. *No* lungs. That comes from eating too much candy."

"That comes from holding my breath," Alina giggled.

"Well, you know, you'll be thinking you're a doctor next...instead of being a mother." Doc gave Alina a wise old look, as if he knew everything.

"No, not at all, silly Doc. Doesn't getting to be a doctor take a lot of time, and money, too, at college?"

"You're quite right about that," agreed Doc Thompson, helping her to the floor from the examination table. "Now, you get your jumper back on."

"Okay, but it's nice and warm in here." Alina pulled the warm wool dress over her head.

"Your mother says you have a new song," began Doc Thompson.

"Oh, yes, but Mama and Duddy have started acting so funny about all that. I realize I shouldn't have told them."

"Well, doctors know about a lot of things. Maybe if you told me about it, I might be able to help."

"Could you take me to Lincoln, for instance? *That* would help," Alina bartered, sitting down in the chair in front of the doctor's desk.

"Well, I'd have to wait and see about *that.* It's

a long way to Lincoln, you know."

"It isn't either," Alina assured him. "It's about two hours in a..." She paused, her brow furrowing.

"Yes? In a what?" asked Doc Thompson.

"Oh, I was just going to say, 'in a car'."

"All right. Well, suppose you begin at the beginning," urged Doc.

"The beginning of what?"

"Why, the beginning of when you started upsetting your parents, for instance." Doc Thompson frowned at her.

"Well, *you* won't get upset like Mama and Daddy, will you?"

"NO, doctors are supposed to not get upset about much of anything," he reassured her.

"Well, Baby...that is, Little Richard...he was upset because of the noisy old wind. So I went and sang him the windy song. And he quieted down."

"Where did you learn the windy song?"

Alina frowned. "I sang it *before*...sort of. Do you want me to sing it for you?"

"Of course," laughed Doc Thompson. "I always enjoy a good song."

Alina gave a significant, exaggerated pause. Then the melody lifted from her breast. Outside in the reception room Julia winced as she heard the song. She looked nervously at the other mothers waiting with their children. Few heard the rise and fall of the melody which obviously, beautifully, was a lullaby interpretation of a windstorm

At the desk, old Miss Hautman paused in her work, a poised pencil in her mouth. "What a pretty melody," she finally said to Julia. "Isn't that your Alina in there?"

"Yes," Julia replied.

Doc Thompson listened carefully until Alina finished. He looked at the child intently. Her eyes returned his look without wavering.

"So, *before*, you had two babies?" he began.

"Yes, Doc Thompson. Two sons." Alina sat a little more erectly, a little more confidently.

"When was that, child?"

"Well, that was before...before *now*." Alina looked a little worried, the familiar frown creasing her forehead.

"I don't want to press you, Alina. The time probably isn't important."

"I suppose...it was...about fifteen years ago," Alina blurted out. She looked shocked, worried. "That's about two years or so before I was born, isn't it?"

"Well, you're almost thirteen now, my dear, so it seems it works out that way."

"Oh." Alina said.

He then watched as she seemed to shrink beneath the implications, to withdraw into some private area of herself that the doctor, through long experience, knew all children possessed: a private universe which separated one reality from another reality, those selected special realities which fitted the time, the place, and became the foundations for their young and adult lives. He knew it was best to wait.

Finally, Alina lifted her head and looked at him directly. "I'm not really supposed to do that, am I?" she asked.

"Not supposed to do what?"

"Remember things like that."

"Whatever you remember, you remember. We can't help that. The question is...will it do anyone any good?"

"What do you mean?" Alina's voice sounded defeated and confused.

"Well, you see how this upsets your mother.

And there is nothing anyone can do about your two...sons. We don't even know where they are."

"Oh yes I do! They live at 210 Yale Street in Lincoln, Nebraska!"

She stopped, as shocked as was the doctor at the mention of an address. "Yes, that's it. They lived there...once. *I lived there...once.*"

Alina gave Doc a hard look of conviction. His mouth opened, betraying his surprise. She was sitting straighter in the chair, yet more relaxed and poised and held her head with a subtle difference, tilted back and chin raised. Her eyes were usually wide open, but now they were somewhat narrowed, giving her gaze a mature speculative quality. "James Hanks was their father...my husband," Alina continued in a slow, deliberate voice that seemed almost to belong to someone else. "Yes, my husband. Why, he must still be alive, then. I guess you see the problem, here Doctor Thompson. Here I am now with all these memories, and I don't know whether to act thirty, twelve, or eight, and am somehow acting like all three."

Doc Thompson felt a chill, not from fear, but of amazement. It was as though a small but adult woman in a child's jumper was sitting opposite him. His amazement barely had time to register consciously before Alina's eyes suddenly filled with tears; she was definitely only young Alina once more, and sobbing heart-brokenly.

Doc Thompson was on his feet instantly. He moved around the desk, sitting down in the chair next to her, pulling her onto his lap.

"There, there, we don't have to go and cry about it, do we? Your mother will think I've scared you to death."

"Oh, Doc Thompson, I wasn't scared before.

But now I *am* scared!" Alina moaned.

"But what is it? You just go on and tell me. I'm supposed to be able to take anything."

"Oh, I don't know. I keep feeling a cold wind on my face. I know I was happy, and then suddenly I wasn't. Now, I'm worried about the two boys. I wonder if they're all right. I wasn't scared until Mama really began to get so scared. Now I'm scared, and Oakley thinks I'm bats on top of all this."

"Now, now, no need to be scared. It's just something you don't understand yet. Nothing to be scared of in that. There are an awful lot of things that even doctors don't understand."

Doc Thompson patted her head. Alina leaned against his chest. Her tears dried quickly, and after a few moments, she smiled up at him weakly "Well, silly doctor, what are we going to do about all this?"

"Well, silly young woman yourself, what would you like to do?"

"Well, I'd like Mama and Daddy not to get scared," she began.

"I suppose I can fix that a little. Even parents can stand a good talking-to once in a while," he laughed.

"And then..." Alina continued.

"Yes, and then what?"

"...and then I'd like to see my two sons...just once more, just to know they're all right."

At this Doc Thompson frowned. "Well, Alina, that might not be so easy..." He searched for something to say that would end this interlude once and for all. But her look of trust in him stopped him.

"I'll tell you what," he found himself saying, "I'll have a good long talk with your parents. Maybe

I'll even come over to your house tonight. How would you like that?"

"Gosh! You mean make a house call even when nobody is sick?"

"Why, sure. I'll make your Daddy invite me over and maybe I'll even bring Reverend Matthews. But that will be after you've gone to bed, so you can't be there. But I promise we will spend the whole evening talking only about you."

"Wow!" said Alina, brushing at her tear-stained cheeks.

"Now, you run along," said Doc. "Have you stopped crying? We don't want your mother to think I've been beating you."

Doc Thompson walked Alina into the reception room. Several waiting mothers, trying to quiet noisy children, looked at him impatiently. He smiled at them and walked directly to Julia.

"Well, Julia, you have a perfectly healthy young lady to your credit."

"You mean *everything* is all right?" asked Julia, a wan smile trembling at the corners of her mouth.

"Yes, but just step inside with me for a moment," he asked, leading the way without pausing.

"I'll be right back, darling," Julia told Alina.

Julia's hands trembled as she closed the inner office door behind her. She collapsed weakly into the chair in front of Doc's desk. Thompson was busy writing out a prescription.

"Is that for her, Doctor?" asked Julia.

"No, it isn't. It's for you. I think you're going to need it to be calm through the days ahead."

"Oh, what *is* it, what's wrong with..."

"I'm going to be very honest with you, Julia. I've known you, your husband and Alina since all of you were born. Medicine doesn't have all the answers. Alina isn't the first child to be brought to my office with a similar complaint…ah, situation."

"You *can't mean* there have been others?" Julia nearly wailed, sitting upright, and staring at him in disbelief.

"Yes, maybe not quite as poignant or as definite as with Alina now. But all the same, clear enough to have become a difficulty in the family."

"But what are we to do?" begged Julia, once more on the verge of tears.

"Well, I'm going to give you a tranquilizer, first off. You go and get this prescription filled and take it as directed. Tonight, I'll want to come along to your house. I mean to bring Reverend Matthews with me."

"Reverend Matthews?"

"Yes. As I say, medicine doesn't have all the answers, and sometimes spiritual guidance will do more than a dozen doctors."

"But what will Richard say?"

"I'll take care of Richard. In fact, I'll call him as soon as you are gone."

"But…Doc, what did she say to you to make you…believe her?"

"Listen, Julia, I'll be very frank. I don't particularly believe her but her own conviction in this matter is extremely strong. Children often remember, or say they remember, things that can't be explained. Things from the past, other places, other people. Well, that's pretty strange, no doubt about it. All sorts of possibilities to investigate, I suppose. But what I'm concerned about, first and foremost, is Alina. We have to do everything we can not to make this a trauma for her. I've seen other children who've remembered things, rememberings, if you want to call them that. For a day or two, maybe even a few weeks.

But then the memories just fade away on their own, or at least the children stop talking about them."

Julia darted a swift look at him. "Oh...I hope that's how it happens with Alina. This is really awful! It'd look so bad if it got around that she..."

A pencil snapped in Doc Thompson's hands. "I was sort of waiting for that," he said grimly. "Not so good for Mr. and Mrs. Town Lawyer to have a kid that's an embarrassment to them with the neighbors, eh?"

Julia flushed. "Doctor, I didn't mean anything like that..."

Doc shook his head. "Oh, you did! You've got a wonderful little girl who's in some kind of trouble we don't understand." He studied her for a moment. "You're a good woman, Julia, a good mother. A little cold, maybe, a little harsh, and you might look into getting past that. But it seems to me that you just sometimes lose sight of what the important things are. You get to fretting over trifles. All right, enough said about that. Now," he said, rising to his feet, "you just talk normally with her about this if she mentions it. If not, don't talk about it. The main thing is, stay calm. You frighten her when you're frightened. Talk with her...don't judge her against whatever you use to govern your own life."

"Oh, Doc, I hate all this...but I guess you're a godsend."

"Nonsense. Just doing my job. Now you run along, Julia. I'll see you tonight."

Doc sighed; it took him a few moments to recover. He was unnerved, in spite of his long years of experience. But he remembered that he had a full office waiting. Before that, he had to call Richard, and then Reverend Matthews.

Chapter
NINE

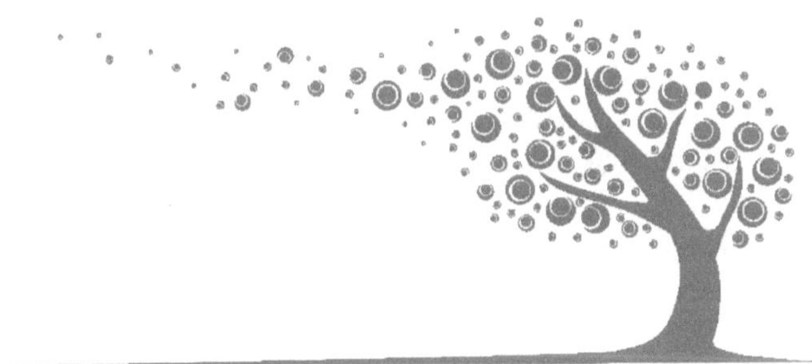

In the car driving home through a light snow flurry with the sun shining boldly anyway, Julia was practicing being calm and normal. She hardly dared to look at Alina since she might break into tears, but she didn't dare not look either. She had to try to be open-minded, loving, and above all, understanding. That was going to be hard.

She looked over at her daughter. Alina was lost in watching the snow collect on what remained of the autumn leaves on the tall poplar trees along the roadside. To her horror, Alina's face was all screwed up, as if in pain. "What is it, honey?" asked Julia, forgetting her own fears.

"I don't *know*, Mama. Something very strange. But I don't want to scare you anymore." Tears then flooded down her cheeks.

"That's...all right, Alina. I talked with Doc Thompson, and I won't be frightened any longer. Well, I'll *try* not to be, if you'll try to help me."

"Yes, Mama. But it's just that the snow on the leaves reminded me of something, like as if there were snow and leaves when..."

"When what?"

"Well, when I died before." The tears still

flowed, but Alina no longer acted as if she was crying, just breathing deeply but calmly.

Julia's hands clenched on the wheel. "Oh, *don't* be scared, Mama," Alina moaned. "I'm sure you won't skid, like that time before."

"*What* time before, Alina?" Julia's voice was almost a wail, and tears blurred her view of the road.

"Well, when the car skidded, and...I got crushed to death..."

"Oh, Alina, Alina..." Julia now wailed. The car swerved a little, but she kept it from running onto the shoulder.

She steadied her voice before she continued. Her tears somehow stopped. Her voice was weak. "We're in this together now, Alina, and we have to be sure of one thing. Whatever it is, it will all turn out all right. We've got to be sure of that. Yes, we have to be sure of that."

"Yes, Mama," agreed Alina.

But there was a faraway look in Alina's eyes, as though she were seeing something unimaginably distant. The reverie lasted only a few seconds. She said gravely, "Yes, Mama, it *will* turn out all right. I somehow know that."

Julia gave a start as Alina, without a pause, said excitedly, "When we get home, can I go over to Oakley's house? Could I stay for dinner? We're going to watch TV, although there's only stupid programs to watch. But there is a special two-hour episode of Star Trek."

"Yes, darling. Anything you want," Julia agreed, relieved. She gave herself a small smile, in spite of her inner turmoil.

She had never thought she'd be glad to have Alina cluttering her mind with TV trash, but it was better than this strange, awful business.

A shutter crossed Julia's shoulders, she hoped Alina wouldn't start talking about it near Oakley's parents. If talk started getting around…

Chapter
TEN

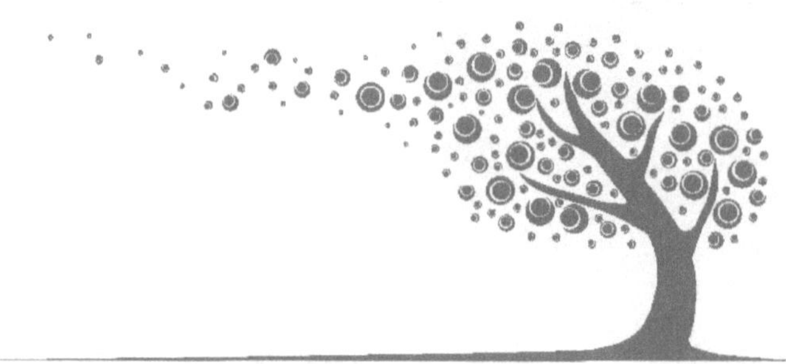

Their bedroom reflected a compromise between Richard's taste for artificial opulence and Julia's hope for intimacy: white rugs, soft grey walls, and warm yellow accents. The somewhat sterile result was, after sundown, leveled toward intimacy by the pink light bulbs Julia employed inside the yellow velour lamp shades.

"The idea," snorted Richard as he fumbled with a brilliantly colored silk tie, "that old Thompson is giving any credence to this thing is almost beyond my understanding." He wound the tie over his hand and pulled it into a loose knot.

"Richard," Julia said, her voice lowered with a rare sound of determination, "I don't think I want any shouting tonight."

"Who's shouting..."

"Your face is flushed."

"I don't care if it is. All this is showing signs of turning into a nightmare. Nothing went right today..."

Julia firmed her lips, calmly fixed an earring, and said nothing.

"Why," Richard continued, a little surprised that he failed to arouse his wife's usual sympathy, "if all this gets around town we'll be a laughingstock for sure."

"If what gets around, Richard?" asked Julia thinly.

"Really, Julia, *really*! You know very well what I mean."

"Well, *really* yourself. I don't know what you *do* mean..."

"That our daughter is...ah, touched."

"Really, Richard!" Julia protested in rising anger, her lower lip trembling. "It's a good thing Alina's gone over to Oakley's house tonight. What if she were here to overhear you say such mean things!"

"Oh, for Chrissakes!" Richard snorted.

"I'll not have you even thinking it," Julia said firmly, almost fiercely, turning from the mirror to face him. Her eyes blazed into his. The glare of a mother protecting her daughter penetrated Richard's masculine umbrage. He opened his mouth, but an instinctual caution prevented words from emerging. The pause was poignant, as if an electrical charge had passed between them. "Julia..." he began.

"I mean it, Richard," she warned again, now softly.

"All this is becoming something I can't understand. This morning you were weepy, begging me to talk to her, to get us over this. Now, well, I just don't understand..."

"Richard, I intend to see this thing through with Alina. I've found out that it *is* a real problem of some sort to her, something that we don't understand."

"Don't tell me that you believe her?"

"I don't *know*, Richard! No, I don't *believe* her exactly. But there *is* something there, something strange and...tender."

"Really, Julia! This morning we...*you* were frightened and in tears over all this. What happened?"

"I talked with Doc Thompson. He said there were...well, sometimes there were other kids with this kind of a...problem."

"I don't believe *that* at all," snarled Richard, pulling on a jacket. "I thought Thompson would get all this over with. Instead he's making it bigger than ever. I'm really very disappointed."

"He *is* a doctor, Richard. He ought to know."

"I don't care about that. He may be a doctor, but he's also an old man now. He's hardly modern, is he?"

Julia began to shake with an inner fury. She pulled her dress over her slip to hide the fury's intensity. "Richard, that old man delivered you, and me, and everyone else in this town, practically. He's never let us down, and he's never been wrong."

"I don't care about all that. He could pass his prime at any moment. Old people do, you know. Old people fail. Their minds, their ability to concentrate...the idea that he could contribute to a child's fantasy, well that's really indicative of senile wandering to me!"

Julia took a deep breath, finishing her dressing. "Children have problems, real problems, Richard. Problems that often are not simply fantasy. Problems that are just as real...and painful, too...as yours are, or mine, for that matter."

"Now don't go throwing up anything at me. I've been good for you, Julia. My problems are important to us both. We have a good marriage."

"A marriage, yes, a marriage," her voice wandered for a moment. "A union, well perhaps not so much."

"Don't go dragging anything else into this mess, damn it. Look, it's like this. I don't think old man Thompson said the right things to you and Alina. It's like this. Down at the office, if there's an issue, the whole staff goes at it until we track it down, and if we can't handle it ourselves, we call in professionals, experts to help."

Julia looked at her husband darkly. "You're talking about calling in a psychiatrist, aren't you? I knew that is just what you would do."

"Come on, Julia. We need help here! Remember when Charlie Bauer's boy went a little crazy and broke all the windows in the school building? Well, he was sent up to Lincoln, to that psychiatrist, Dr. Wollen, who straightened out that little brat soon enough."

"Alina *is not* crazy, Richard. And I'm warning..."

Richard ignored her. "Soon as Thompson called me with his clap trap, I called up Dr. Wollen and explained it all to him. He thought it was an interesting case, and agreed to come down right away. 'She's approaching puberty,' he said, 'and her hormones might get a little haywire.' It'll cost plenty, of course, but he seems to be the best here in Nebraska."

"Richard! A psychiatrist ought to be the last recourse, not the first. I think you're very premature." Julia's voice was icy as she turned her back on her husband.

Richard was stunned by her sudden distance. He faltered, groping for words. "Julia, what's really happened since this morning? You were mighty scared this morning about how Alina was acting. I didn't say that Wollen is the key, but It's stupid to let that meddling Thompson pull this out of proportion. And that young minister! That stupid revolutionary this town has acquired. Julia, we *have* to get in someone who'll help us sort all this out."

"We could try ourselves, first, Richard, before we hire other people to tend our family for us."

Richard blanched, sucking in air. He drew back from his wife. He groped for new words, his voice rose in pitch, in terror almost. "Julia, I don't care what you think. I simply won't have any of this! I won't let old man Thompson say it might be true! I don't trust our new young Reverend Matthews! I have to put my faith in common sense! We have to have a professional here. *That's* common sense!"

"Richard, what *is* the matter with you? What are you talking about, taking Alina to Doc Thompson was *your* idea."

Richard looked around the room for help. There was none to be found in the emotionless walls. He wrinkled his brow. "Julia," he said in tight anger, exhaling with controlled effort, "I simply cannot believe in all this reincarnation garbage!"

The word fell heavily on both of them. It was as if an ancient bell tolled across the Nebraska prairies, a strange bell, cloaked within the folds of the winter winds. The meaning replete within the word came and went and passed soundlessly.

Julia moved to her husband and found herself leaning against him.

He spoke first, "We'd better go downstairs."

Richard," she murmured softly, almost momentously, "They'll probably all here already."

Chapter
ELEVEN

By pure coincidence, yet perhaps summoned by time and eternity, the three divergent consultants arrived together. Cold wind and wandering snowflakes invaded the entrance hall as the group came indoors -- having made their introductions amongst themselves while still outside.

"The sun was shining up in Lincoln when I left there," commented Dr. Wollen glumly, making straight for the warm fireplace in the living room.

Doc Thompson smiled at the squat burley psychiatrist: "That is typical Nebraska weather! Always unpredictable! Like human nature," he said aloofly.

The young Reverend Matthews smiled at the jibe, but said nothing.

"Could you gentlemen use something warm?" began Richard, failing to conceal his discomfort. "You don't mean cocoa, I hope?" Doc Thompson teased. "The weather calls for a little *spiritus frumenti* you know, something to warm the soul as well as the body."

"I had scotch in mind, Thompson," said Richard.

"I'd prefer bourbon, if you have it," Doc

retorted.

Dr. Wollen nodded, too, as did Reverend Matthews who said, "It's really has turned suddenly into bourbon weather, hasn't it, Dr. Wollen?"

"I always drink bourbon, no matter the weather," commented Wollen dryly, his eyes avoiding Matthews.

Richard gritted his teeth at Julia, who smiled primly as she arranged glasses on a tray. The entire scene, now from its start, was already theatrically artificial, as if the players were trying to avoid a tragedy by way of trivialities. Julia sat to one side while the four men talked animatedly of the changing weather, past winters on the Nebraskan prairies, the heavy winds and deep snows, and the tragedies that had taken place years back.

The bantering went on until, amid the weather and old tales, Doc Thompson launched into the real topic. "Old Reverend Andrews and I," he said, swirling ice cubes in his glass, "in years gone by often had to deal with situations similar to this one." Now no one else hardly dared to breathe, and only the snapping fire could be heard. "Old Andrews," Doc went on, "well he would have started by exhibiting a great deal of sympathy about such a memory, get it all out, then begin a soft lecture that gradually built up in power and strength, until the child was convinced that it was unthinkable that it should be mentioned ever again. Fear…well, old Andrews knew how to install it, how to change it, how to alleviate it, if necessary. The few children who occasionally had such memories never clung to them awfully long after Andrews had got through with them."

Now no one else spoke for a few moments. "As I understand it," then said Reverend Matthews,

"Alina says she has certain memories…ah, can we call them that?" He looked questioningly at the members of the gathering. Richard and Julia looked back meekly at him.

Dr. Wollen cleared his throat. "There could be any number of explanations for this occurring in the child. However, I would have to talk with Alina quite a while before I could make an adequate diagnosis."

Both Matthews and Thompson glared openly at Wollen, whose manner was brusque and defiantly authoritative. "It's not a diagnosis that's our problem," Thompson snorted. "The problem is how to get Alina past this confusion, and into a more usual perspective for her age. Experience has taught me that children can get past this when it occurs. Frankly, Richard, I'm disappointed that you saw fit to invite a psychiatrist into what is probably only a passing fancy on Alina's part."

Richard was not to be put down. "And I'm somewhat disappointed you saw fit to invite Matthews here. I can't see how any of this should be extended into his realms of interests or concerns or his far-out ideas that have everyone talking whether he is even suitable for our town…well…"

At this Julia broke into crying, tears squeezing from her closed eyes while she lifted quivering hands to wipe them away without spoiling her mascara.

"Julia, did you fill that prescription?" asked Doc Thompson. Julia sniffed and looked straight at him, regaining herself quickly.

"I appreciate your concern, Doc Thompson, but in the car driving home, Alina started talking about her last…death. I decided not to stop at the drug store."

"I think you might see to that at once, then," suggested Thompson pointedly.

"No, I won't. I've thought about all this and *really* If I can't support my daughter through this without the aid of tranquilizers, then I'm not much of a mother, am I?" She looked at the men defiantly.

Richard scrutinized her impersonally, distantly. "Well, Julia, then stop crying. We can't talk about this through your usual veil of tears." Julia's eyes blazed.

Reverend Matthews stepped into the breach. "Did you say her past death?" he asked.

"Yes...she said that it had just started snowing, like now, when she...died before. She was so changed, her voice different, almost a different person than my little Alina. I couldn't help but wonder..."

"Julia, mothers are wrong to sympathize," interrupted Dr. Wollen. "Children often construct fantasies around present-time events. They take the present and weave parts of it into their fantasy life..."

"Fantasies seldom come equipped with specific addresses in other towns," Thompson said testily. "By any chance, Dr. Wollen, is there a Yale Street in Lincoln?"

"There may be Thompson. If so, however, I've no patients living on it." Wollen forced a chuckle. "But to address myself to your point, Doctor, psychological literature provides many cases of remarkably detailed and consistent fantasies, complete enough with 'facts' to convince a jury. A jury of laymen, at least."

Doc Thompson looked at the psychiatrist steadily in spite of the pointed put-down. "Well, I don't know that I'd be happy in calling what Alina is experiencing merely a fantasy. There have been a few other children hereabouts, through the years..."

Richard looked at him in dismay; Wollen with patronizing amusement. "Dr. Thompson," Wollen interrupted, "am I, are we, all here tonight to conclude that the principal medical man in this small township accepts that some children actually can remember lives lived before? Why, this is preposterous, and especially so from a man of medicine!"

Thompson flushed hotly, but his voice remained calm. "I suppose you are inferring that I'm a country quack. You might just go to hell, for all I care. These are modern times, Dr. Wollen. Psychiatry has proven to be far from the panacea of the mind that it was once thought. Even here in the prairies we manage to keep up. I might inform you that for every inadequacy in psychiatry to explain the average human, there are advances elsewhere, in parapsychology, for instance..."

"Oh, really!" protested Wollen, cutting him off.

"Gentlemen...doctors," Reverend Matthews began smoothly, "I don't think we have met here to argue whether this is a psychological problem of a parapsychological event. These are advancing times, and there is plenty of evidence to support either claim."

"I don't understand what you mean?" said Richard, happy to have Wollen and Thompson quieted, as he regarded the young Reverend with steel-cold eyes, nevertheless.

"Why, simply that even though it *is* strange to consider, we in divinity schools are forced to assume that there may be more to spirit and soul than has been thought. We study parapsychology today, and..."

"Reverend Matthews," Richard protested, "are you suggesting that we actually give credence to my daughter's ...uh, fantasies!"

"Actually, yes, that is, unless you've already made up your mind as to what Alina's problem really is."

Richard's mouth dropped open. "Well, I have called in Dr. Wollen to determine that, Reverend Matthews. I didn't invite you here tonight," his gazed shifted towards the doctor. "Our family doctor took that on himself. As far as I am concerned, I give to the church, I respect religion, but I don't appreciate missionary zeal in my own living room, especially from an untried young minister with unusual ideas."

"I apologize if I am offensive, Richard. I am a rebel, that's true. Religion is changing, and I may or may not have a mission, a calling in old terms. But there are two things I would like to point out. First, Alina is, as are you, a member, an individual, in my parish. I should like to be of service if I can. But secondly, I don't believe I want to have a case of open reincarnation in my back yard here. There would be newspapers, investigators, all kinds of negative repercussions. I've seen this happen before. Your daughter will talk, believe me, at least to her young friends. They will confide in their mothers; the gossip will start. Could you not set aside your dislike of me, the unfamiliarity of the situation, so that we might create a line of thought on this..."

Doc Thompson broke out laughing. Reverend Matthews looked at him in amazement. "Don't mind me, Reverend," Thompson chuckled. "I just had a picture of old Reverend Andrews. He must be turning in his grave at the moment. He simply would have told Alina that she was possessed by the devil and ordered her not to talk about it at all. He ruled this town by religious terror, the old country method of keeping everyone in church, I believe. Now, though, *you* don't refer to the devil, but still want the same thing Andrews did...a clean back yard. Well! It seems the times change, but the goals don't."

"Well," Matthews resumed, "all that aside, my point is that giving credence to anything at all, except Alina's problem would be beside the point. We have not really asked her if she has a problem! She may not find her fantasy or memory problematical, you know."

Julia suddenly interrupted with a giggle. The four men turned to her with mixed expressions.

"Really, Julia, I don't see..." Richard began.

"Oh, Richard!" Julia laughed, relieved. "It's just struck me that *our* confusions, *our* problem, is somewhat larger to us than Alina's is to her."

Richard's face froze. "Don't be foolish, Julia. Sometimes you remind me too much of my nutty sister, Margaret. She's the one always carrying on about spirits and ghosts and things."

Julia faced her husband calmly. "Margaret has nothing at all to do with this. Perhaps you'd better offer another round of drinks, Richard."

Chapter
TWELVE

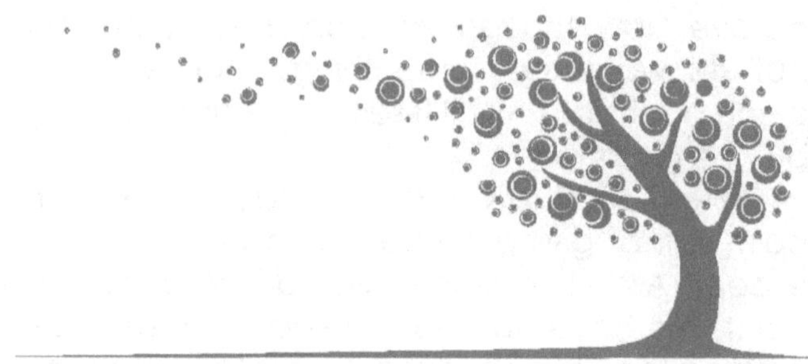

Sprawled on the floor in the basement rumpus room, Oakley's attention was riveted on the flickering screen of the TV. Alina's gaze was fixed on some distant point beyond the ceiling.

"When I grow up," groaned Oakley in the throes of participative ecstasy, "I'm going to be a star pilot!"

"An astronaut, dummy," murmured Alina.

"Oh, fig anyway! There's no difference between a star pilot and an astronaut."

"Yes, I suppose not..."

"Honestly, dummy," Oakley teased, "I don't know where you are *at* these days, all the time gazing at things in your mind. I bet you're going crazy, or something."

"Yeah, probably," agreed Alina distantly.

"Oh, rats! I can't even talk to you anymore," Oakley protested, concentrating once again on the TV.

"TV is really boring, compared to real life, don't you think?" asked Alina.

"Most certainly not! Real life is dull, dull, dull!"

"Do you remember things from before you were born?"

"Gosh, no. Who does? I don't even remember

being born. Besides, I feel like I came to earth on a spaceship."

"*In* a spaceship, dummy, not on one. You would have exploded in empty space."

"Yeah, I suppose so," Oakley agreed, her face screwed up at the thought.

"I remember something from before I was born," confessed Alina suddenly, in a different voice. Oakley ceased watching the TV to look suspiciously at Alina.

"I had children and everything..."

"Oh, you're such a liar. No one can remember things like that..."

"I can too! And it wasn't very long ago, up in Lincoln. I remember it all...or most of it."

"You're just as crazy as your aunt, but I'll try to love you nevertheless," said Oakley with dramatic charity.

"I've decided to go and see them, too..."

"Who?"

"My children..."

"Dummy..."

"Will you come with me?"

"Where?"

"Up to Lincoln."

"Stupid! That's not just like going across town to the shopping mall."

"Well, I've got to go. I've got to know. I don't care about anything else, except to see if they were taken care of."

"Who?"

"I just told you. My two sons, that's who!"

"Well, I promise I won't tell."

"Tell what?"

"That you're *possessed*..."

"Possessed by who?"

"By a ghost, stupid, like your aunt."

"Oh, rats, you stupid thing! I can't talk to you at all anymore." Alina jumped over and tackled Oakley, who rolled and squealed in pleasure until they bumped the TV set, whose face turned into lines and waves.

"Now look what you've done," Oakley complained. "Daddy says never to fiddle with the set. The repairman *costs!*"

"It's all so wonderful," sighed Alina, paying no attention.

"What is so wonderful?"

"Memory, stupid. It's like having a head full of long-distance waves, going out in all directions. All I have to do is follow any one of them. Then, they turn into pictures, all sorts of pictures, like colored ribbons with real bits of life attached to their ends." Her voice shifted in quality, wandering.

Oakley surveyed her for a few silent moments. "Sometimes you really scare me, you know. Sometimes you sound like you're a different person…I prefer imagination to memory, and I'm not even old yet."

"Yes, imagination…like Daddy and Mama. Everything is imagination to them! I'm afraid I've given them a problem…"

"I think that's *utterly fair*," Oakley said, giggling but somehow also seriously. "It's only fair because parents give us so many problems, don't you think?"

"Uhm, I suppose so. Daddy, well Daddy is really very impatient, and he sure is scared of memories."

"Well, so am I, you dummy. You better help me fix this TV set before *my* Daddy comes down here and starts yelling."

"Fix it yourself. It's your TV. I'm going home and try to find out if Jim Hanks still lives in Lincoln…"

"Who?"

"My last husband, dummy…"

"Oh, honestly! You are flying around like a bat!"

Chapter
THIRTEEN

Helping himself to more *spiritus frumenti*, Doc Thompson filled his glass and then turned to the group: "In my experience whatever the truth in the memories, or the fantasy, it is usually that the child is worried about something or someone left behind, a loved one perhaps."

"Yes, indeed, like dolls, puppies and goblins," chastised Dr. Wollen.

Julia stood up and nervously, doing her best to hide her anger, and began straightening the clutter of glasses and cigarette buts off the coffee table. "I think you are being a little rude, Dr. Wollen," she said quietly. Her icy tone was very polite.

Wordlessly, Wollen stiffened in his chair, looked questioningly at Richard, who offended nothing other than an apologetic shrug.

Thompson went on. "Once these worries are alleviated, the, uh, the *trauma*, the fantasy, the memories, well, they all seem to pass away. The child seems to forget. After all, once we grownups are assured that our loved ones, after they have passed on, are in Heaven, we forget all about them, or at least mostly so."

"Your reverse logic doesn't hold water for me,"

Richard said glumly.

"For me either," agreed Wollen. "Your country wisdom might produce results, Dr. Thompson, but actually what proof, what research data, do you have that in using this approach you have assured a non-neurotic future for the children who have claims like this? You must know that it's totally irresponsible to *reinforce* fantasies!"

"Then why, why, Dr. Wollen," Julia asked coldly, "are our entire lives composed almost totally of fantasies, of dreams, of fictions..."

"Julia," said Richard firmly, "I wish you would sit down and shut up. You're not helping..."

"Go to hell, Richard!" she retorted hotly. "Life, living, is composed of more than just facts and figures, you know!"

Richard exhaled and retreated visibly from Julia's impassioned words. He turned stiffly to Wollen. "I'd be very interested in what you might recommend, Dr. Wollen," he indicated softly, but with cold determination, "since if Alina does not stop this...this...whatever it is, I fully intend to put her under your care."

"Richard!" Julia said in open dismay. "She's only *twelve*! What would the people in town say if they found out we needed a psychiatrist for our daughter when she's only *twelve*?!"

Wollen cleared his throat. "Well, as I said, I couldn't make a diagnosis until I had talked, at the very least, in some length, with Alina. But there are several approaches. I might look into wish fulfillment, for instance. Perhaps she has a powerful wish to supplant her mother in her father's eyes. I notice the occurrence of two children in her fantasy. Richard, you have two children. This often happens when a baby comes along. The elder child sees it as competition for attention."

"Yes," agreed Richard, nodding his head. "That might make sense..."

Julia's hands tightened on the chair arms. Doc Thompson pursed his lips, hiding his impatience by taking a drink and rolling his eyes.

"Then," continued Wollen, his words lacking any color, "there are repressed memories of someone she might have known in the present. There's always hypnagogic reverie to be considered, that is, a dream continuing into the waking states, and being embellished upon by fantasy. These images often become very possessive..."

"And," Reverend Matthews interrupted, "you might include screen memories."

Wollen looked at him blankly.

"Yes, Dr. Wollen," said Reverend Matthews without smiling, "I have a degree in psychology, also."

"What are screen memories?" Richard asked.

Reverend Matthews continued, cutting Wollen's effort to explain. "They are memories or imagined sequences put up as a defense or as a screen against something the person doesn't want to confront or acknowledge. We all, that is most of us, tend to use screen memories. We tend to think of things through screens. Mostly these are created by the mind to screen out things we don't want to see or believe. They form a lot of our reactions to things."

"We're not talking of screen memories, here, Reverend," Wollen stated with some anger. "We are talking of a delusion, one powerful enough to create havoc in an ordinary family! A delusion powerful enough to delude others! A delusion powerful enough to convert others into belief in it."

"Is that what you are worried about?" asked Thompson, not even trying to hide his wide grin. "Are you afraid that Alina might win, uh, *converts* to the possibility of having lived before. Well, I do say! That would really create havoc in psychiatry, wouldn't it?"

Wollen grasped for a retort, but failed to locate the proper words. He took a long swig of his drink instead.

Reverend Matthews smiled. "Well," he said, as in concluding a sermon of his own, "it would probably create havoc in everything. Our minds are not really prepared for anything beyond the physical at all. If it were possible that the soul transcends death, that is one thing. But that it transcends bodies, that it might move from body to body, well that is totally another...."

"Those are old, outdated, irrational concepts, Reverend," Wollen almost shouted.

"We only know that they are *old* concepts. They are held as irrational by psychiatry, not by human people in general. We do not know yet that they are irrevocably irrational, Dr. Wollen, that is, unless you are claiming infallible omniscient knowledge about everything."

The heaviness of the young man's words seemed to settle through the living room, casting a cloak over the argument.

"I see," mused Thompson quixotically, "that we, in our wisdom, have once more reached the brink of philosophy..." If *he* smiled, no one else did.

The outside wind breathed through the house, emphasizing the eternalness of the confrontation.

Chapter
FOURTEEN

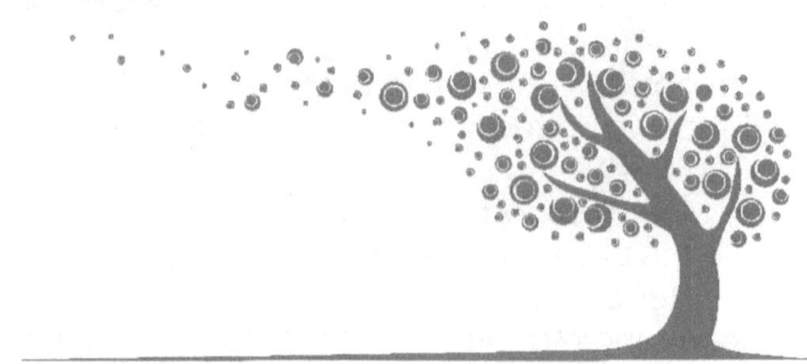

Alina walked slowly up to the house. The sighing arras of the wind seemed to enfold the house in an island of security that gleamed warm golden streamers from the windows into the outside, leaving trails of light across the cold boards of the back porch.

Climbing the steps, she leaned against the balustrade, contemplating the nighttime stars above. She was startled momentarily by a dark shadow that moved up the walk. Aunt Margaret was bundled up warmly, a vast hood pulled about her face.

"Is that you, Aunt Margaret?" Alina giggled. "You look like a magician coming out of the night."

"Whatever are you doing out here in the cold?" Margaret asked, hugging the girl.

"Oh, I don't know. I was watching the stardust out there in the universe. It's all so beautiful, the stars, the blowing nighttime clouds. The moon's going to rise shortly. Don't you see the light there on the eastern horizon?"

"Yes, indeed. It'll be almost full tonight." Margaret drew her niece closer. "Here, we don't want you to catch an early cold. They tend to hang on, you know. You should really be inside."

"Oh, I expect so. They're in there yelling about me, I suppose. I can hear them now and then. I didn't feel like going in to all *that*. I know I've upset Daddy something awful. He's got a doctor from Lincoln, a si-ky-a-trist, in there. They're discussing the possibility that I'm crazy. I've been listening at the window."

"Naughty girl. Eavesdropping..."

"No, not really. I just couldn't *help* but hear them when I came back from Oakley's house."

"A psychiatrist? Are you sure?"

"Yep. And Doc Thompson and that Reverend Matthews, too. I guess I made a mistake when I told them about my babies from before. Daddy got red in the face, and he's still that way. Mama's been yelling at *him*...she hardly ever does that, and in front of all those others, too. So I thought I'd contemplate the stars for a while, and perhaps they would all leave."

"Well, you are too young to contemplate the stars, my dear, when it's too cold out here. Why don't we go in and see what's going on?"

"Yes, I suppose so...Aunt Margaret, why do you suppose I wasn't your daughter instead of Mama's? I'd much rather it were that way."

"Hush, child. Your mother loves you deeply. You shouldn't think such things."

"I'd much rather live with you, even though I'm not supposed to *think* about anything at all."

"My poor dear, it's true. Thinking gets one in all sorts of trouble, and opening your mouth about your thoughts is really quiet dangerous."

"Why didn't you have children?"

"Well, I don't know, exactly. Your Uncle Ned and I tried to have one, but it never worked, for some reason. I guess no one wanted us..."

"But are you sterile or something?"

"My goodness, you *are* really getting grown up, aren't you?"

"No, silly. We learn about such things in school nowadays. *Were* you sterile or something?"

"No, not at all. Neither was your Uncle Ned. We just simply were never blessed, that's all. Perhaps it was me, in some way. All I ever wanted was your Uncle Ned. I loved him from first sight, as if we'd known each other for an eternity, as if we were drawn together..."

"Like two magnets, maybe?"

"Well, better than *that*. Maybe, down deep, he and I didn't really want another to come between us. Just he and I. Some loves are like that. It seemed sufficient. At any rate, even though we tried, we never conceived a child. We thought we should try, but we were never really disappointed when it didn't work out, either."

"Hum...there's so much I don't understand. Except I wish I was your child, instead of Mama's and Daddy's. They're really so ex-as-per-ating, you know."

"My dear, you know you love your parents."

Yes, but I love you better. Daddy doesn't really seem human, more like a machine..."

"You shouldn't talk that way. Your Daddy, well, he's uncomfortable in life, and he compensates for that discomfort by trying to be hard. I remember when you were born. They had wanted a child for years. He was so pleased when you came, and he wouldn't let anyone else hold you for days after."

"But he treats me like...well, I don't know, but not like a *person*!"

"He's just confused. Most parents, I think, find it a difficult time when their child starts turning into a real person. They want them to be just like themselves. But everyone is an individual. Your Mama and Daddy will grow with you...if you give them a chance. But, I do declare, all this talking you're doing about babies *from before* must be very difficult for them. It might not be true, you know, only a dream you had."

"That's *not* so at all! I know it's true. I *want* it to be true."

"But, little Alina, we don't always get what we want. That's a rule of life, and understanding that is part of growing up."

"I don't care! It *is* true! And that's all there is to it. And I'm going to go up to Lincoln and see if my two sons have been cared for, even if I have to hitchhike myself!"

Margaret held her niece close. "Well, I see we do have a real problem here. I suppose I was wrong to tell you about my memories, my deep memories. They may have been only my imagination way back then. I was always too imaginative, all my life. That irritated even your Uncle Ned many times."

"I don't care, Aunt Margaret," said Alina pulling away from the warm cuddle. "None of this is *your* fault. It's no one's *fault*. I know love endures. I know it is never really lost. Maybe it wanders among the stars. But I think love *is* love, and I really think I love my memory of my two babies more than Mama and Daddy love me."

Margaret's lips quivered. Tears formed in her eyes.

"Silly Aunt Margaret. Don't *you* cry, too! The cold wind will freeze your eyes shut!"

"True, true," Margaret sighed, talking deep breaths. "Well, little one, even if you're prepared to contemplate the stars all night, I'm getting cold myself. Let me take you in now."

"Okay. But tomorrow morning...I'm going to find a bus schedule and see how to get up to Lincoln. I *know* they are still there...but, of course, they are much older by now."

"Oh, dear..." Margaret groaned, opening the screen door. Warm light covered their two dark shapes as they entered the house, and entered, too, into the sounds of voices cascading from the living room.

Chapter
FIFTEEN

A strong reverie had entered Dr. Wollen and he found his tooting: "Our very biased way of thinking is unscientific, and as to who might possess omniscient knowledge, Reverend Matthews, I think *you* must have pretenses to that. What else are churches other than bastions of pretended omniscient, all-assuming knowledge? In my opinion, which is scientifically supported, all religious ministries are merely cases of teen-age hysteria, hysteria that is extended into a quasi-professional calling…"

Julia was unable to contain herself. She leapt to her feet, hovering over Richard. "This is disgusting!" she shouted. Richard sank back into his chair. "Are you seriously considering entrusting our daughter to this man? This…this hideous creature who thinks he has all the solutions in his pocket…"

Richard recovered from the sudden outburst, and rose to his own feet. "Yes, Julia, I *am* considering doing just that! I will not have my family torn apart by a fantasy." He drew himself erect. "There can't possibly be anything such as a past life! I have to cling to that fact…"

"That's *not* a fact, Richard. It's only a scientific

assumption..."

"What's gotten into you, Julia? This morning..."

"I don't care about this morning. I only care about now! About the fact that you're going to hand Alina over to this mind-shaper, this bombastic fool..."

"Julia! You're acting like a fool yourself! Why, I've never seen you like this!"

"That may be true, Richard. But I'll not stand for you giving our daughter, Alina, over to this...this psychiatric idiot!"

"Oh yes you will! You *will!* You have no other choice!"

"Damn you, Richard! I'll fight you on this! I've never fought you on anything before. But I'll fight on this!"

Richard reeled and backed away from his wife. Astonishment wrinkled his brow. "You can fight all you want," he said quietly. "But I intend to see that Alina is straightened out, and that's final."

Julia faced her husband defiantly for a moment. But the tears then broke through. She collapsed into her chair in sobs. Richard stared down at her dispassionately. Ignoring Thompson and Matthews, he faced Dr. Wollen. "What kind of arrangements have to be made, Doctor?" he asked emptily.

None of them had noticed Alina and older woman with her who had silently appeared in the dining room doorway. Margaret's expression showed astonishment at the scene. Alina's gaze seemed to go right through everyone.

Alina spoke before Wollen could answer her father. Her words, the deepened voice, both so foreign, silenced everyone.

"Daddy," she said, her young body drawn erect, seemingly taller, "that will be enough. I shall be satisfied to let all this go when I find out how my two sons have been cared for."

Even her aunt found herself looking down with surprise at her niece, almost suddenly someone else other than little Alina. Julia hesitated only a moment, then dashed across the room, across the stunned silence of the four men. She drew her daughter into her arms, crying openly and freely.

"And I," she cried aloud, "will help you find out! If your memories prove not to be true, then I'll help you resolve all that, too!"

Chapter
SIXTEEN

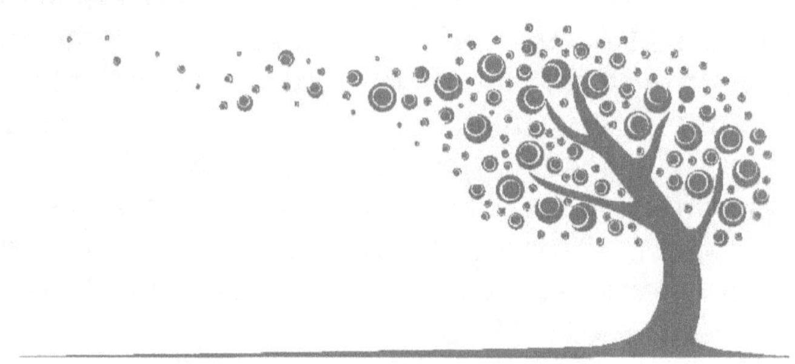

Now, one by one, as if popping up like jacks, the gentlemen rose from their seats, in politeness perhaps to Richard's elder sister, but also visibly shaken by Alina's poise and manner. Richard, recovering from his obvious shock, cleared his throat. "Alina, I think you should go upstairs. What we are talking about here doesn't concern you."

"Richard!" wailed Julia, "how can you say that?"

"I intend to do what is best for the girl, Julia," Richard said rigidly, his shoulders beginning to shake, "and she's too young to understand what's going on here, and too young to know what's best for her."

"Richard," Margaret began...

"And I'll thank you to leave, Margaret," Richard said coldly. "I suspect that it's your mystic vapors that have turned Alina's head, anyway."

Margaret drew up in a gasp, white hurt pinching her face. "I'll not have you ordering your own sister from *my* house," Julia said, advancing on Richard. "I have never known you to be such a tyrant, Richard! Cold, unpassionate..."

"Unpassionate?" gasped Richard.

"Yes, unfeeling, cold, distant...truly uncaring!"

"Julia! How can you, in front of these men..."

Alina burst into tears and hugged her mother tighter. Her voice was again the Alina they all knew. "Mama, don't let me make you fight with Daddy..."

"It's all right, honey. Sometimes things need to be said..."

"I'll go, Richard," Margaret interrupted, coming up out of her hurt, "but not before I've said something..."

"I don't want you to say anything..."

"You'll hear me out," Margaret said, walking toward him. "You *are* cold, and unfeeling, too, and I don't particularly care. It's your life. Still I know how you feel about Alina..."

"How *could* you know? You've never had a child."

"That doesn't matter. I know how grateful you were when Alina came along. I can sense your deep love for her. But don't you think you hide it, hide that love, too well? You will never solve life's problems by holding yourself uninvolved from them, in the way...in the way you draw up papers to foreclose on a farmer hereabouts, when his crops fail."

"How dare you!" breathed Richard in black rage.

"I dare! I may never come into this house again, nor might I ever care to. But you can't treat Alina like you treat matters of law. Simple-minded legal arguments at that, as far as this town's concerned."

Richard backed away from his sister, raising his fists to his cheeks. Margaret advanced upon him.

"Sending Alina to this psychiatrist will not help in the long run...you know very well that he'll end up putting her on some kind drug or something, anything simply to make her forget or be insensitive to her own thoughts. He doesn't know anything about past lives! How, then, can you expect him to deal with..."

"You don't know anything about such matters..."

"It won't help, because...don't you see, Alina's soul is bigger than yours, than his, maybe bigger than all of ours put together. You ask how I dare? How dare *you*, in your conscience, to try to limit her, to reduce her, to your level."

"I'll not listen to this occult garbage," Richard screamed, looking toward Wollen for help. But Wollen was pale and mute.

"This isn't occult garbage, Richard, but simply observation!" Margaret, without losing a step continued, "look at Alina..."

Everyone was forced to look at the child who had remained immobile, as if frozen by the anger about her.

"Look at her! Don't you see? She has memories of roots that we don't have, a love we all have missed, possibilities that go beyond these empty, unmerciful prairies." She paused. There was no sound. She looked around expectantly. But those in the room were frozen.

"I know what you think of me, Richard. I've never tried to change that, since I've not really cared. I had my life, and it was good, which is more than most people hereabouts can claim."

"Oh, Margaret," breathed Julia, leaving Alina and going up to the older woman instead, her arms reaching out.

"No, Julia, don't. You really belong to Richard, and I'll now promise never to come into his house again. But I beg you, Richard, let Alina work this out for herself. She has substance that you haven't recognized, and I truly believe…" Margaret broke into tears…"that somehow she has known life more than any of us here." She wiped her eyes with her hands, pulling the hood up. "I'll go now…"

Reverend Matthews took her hand. "My dear, dear woman," he began softly. "Don't mind for me, young man," Margaret stated proudly. "You just come along and get the apple sauce you wanted. It's ready and waiting."

She turned once more. "I...I have to go home now…Ned is waiting for me somewhere, and I only wish we had gone on together..."

She left the warm room. A moment later the back screen-door slammed shut, but before it did, the prairie winds wailed briefly through the hallway.

Chapter
SEVENTEEN

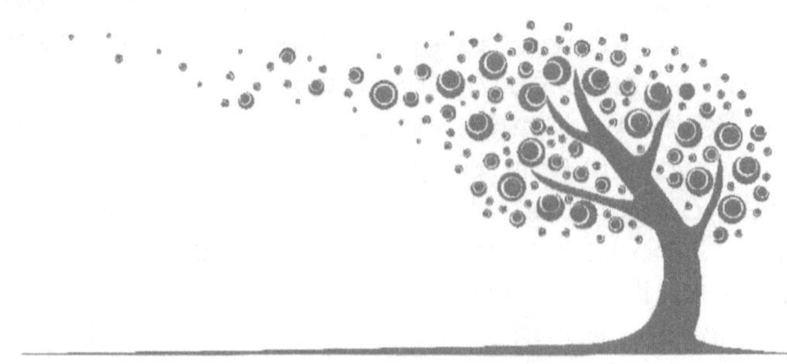

Alina was the first to break the troubled silence left in the wake of her aunt's disquieting departure. "Daddy," she said, "tomorrow I'm going to go up to Lincoln. I got to go see..."

"You'll do no such thing!" Richard roared at her. Alina quailed before his fury, but only slightly so. Her body shook, seeming torn in two directions at once.

Julia, now returned to her daughter's side, pulled her closely into her arms. "Now see what you've done," she accused.

Alina's eyes rolled in her head, her teeth biting down on her lower lip.

"Oh, Alina, darling, what's the matter?" wailed Julia.

Dr. Wollen quickly crossed the room, taking the girl's hand into his, feeling for a pulse.

At his touch Alina's eyes opened narrowly, her body stopped trembling. Her lips seemed to grow fuller, a rosy color inundating her pale face. "It's all right, Mama," she said, but in a deep, melodious voice issuing from the mouth that only moments before had belong to little Alina, but now did not. Wollen drew back with a gasp. Julia's eyes widened. Doc Thompson bent over the small girl's body.

"I know," Alina began, "all this is painful to you, to all of you. I'm terribly sorry." She disengaged herself from her mother's arms and walked to a chair and sat primly on its edge.

"Alina?" probed Richard, weakly.

"Of course, I'm still your daughter."

"Good God!" murmured Doc Thompson, drawing closer to the girl, "listen to the voice! It's *not* Alina's."

"Silly, kind doctor Thompson," Alina smiled, but her big grey eyes now began taking on additional depth, emotion, comprehension. Minute changes went through her, small shudders that all could see.

Julia drew back, but Reverend Matthews came closer, bending down on his knees. Alina looked at him levelly, without fear. Then, the depth of her voice flooded through the room.

"I fully realize that none of you understand. Now that I have remembered them, I must go and see them, my two sons. You may or may not wish to help me, but I shall go..."

"Alina," begged Richard. "Alina, don't do this to me..." His hand shook as he held it out to his daughter. Alina drew back, upright from his offered hand. Richard jerked it back, hurt. "Damn you, then," he breathed softly.

"Richard, can't you see," breathed Julia. "This is not our Alina..."

"Don't be foolish," he snarled. But he looked at Alina...

"She's speaking from beyond the grave," offered Doc Thompson in awe.

"Don't be daft, Doc Thompson," the voice giggled. "I *am* here, right in front of you. Hardly from beyond the grave."

"You're a mighty good actress for your age," laughed Dr. Wollen uncomfortably.

"That may be, but everything need not be an act. I understand why you are here; I understand why Daddy asked for you. This must be extremely difficult for a man...of his nature. I know it was wrong in talking about it. But I did. And now it's too late. What must be done, I have to do."

Reverend Matthews was the only one to find his voice, and even then he could hardly speak through his incredulity. "Wrong? Wrong about what?"

"In speaking of my death. I understand now that one should not do that. It's unfair..."

"Unfair?"

"Yes, unfair. People want to think in terms of life, of living..."

"But then," Thompson interrupted, "you're not Alina now?"

"Yes, of course I am. But my memories are from Helena."

"Helena?" gasped Richard.

"Yes."

"You mean that person? Isn't that what you said in my office this afternoon?" asked Doc Thompson, getting hold of himself.

"Silly doctor. I *am* that person, Helena Hanks...and I'm myself, too."

"I can't believe any of this," Richard said, collapsing on the couch, his eyes riveted on Alina. Julia moved to sit beside him. He reached out for her. She gathered herself into his arms, tears freely flowing.

"Do you really remember?" asked Reverend Matthews simply.

"Of course. Isn't that what this is all about? Not

everything, of course. But they are definitely there, those old, those old *real* memories. It's surprising they cause fear in you all. There's no fear in them for me, at least for now."

"There was fear before?" Matthews asked.

Alina's face tightened. "Yes, before, when the memories weren't clear enough, and fear, too, at that dreadful moment...There was the cool wind on my face, the sounds of Jim's laughter. The feeling of happiness. I had just found out I was pregnant, for the third time. We were so happy. The cool wind coming in the car window. The yellow leaves on the trees, the light snow falling on them. My thoughts...I am always so happy when I'm pregnant. I hope it's a girl this time. After all, two boys is enough. Jim is so fulfilled. He always worried he couldn't have any more children after he came back from the war. Why, I'll never know. He's ultra-passionate, demanding, in excess sometimes. There's the stop sign. Oh, he's missing it...there's the other car coming..." Alina's voice quavered.

There was no other sound in the room, except for the remaining interspaced crackles of the fireplace. "There's that car coming! Oh, why did Jim miss the stop sign? It's coming...my side of the car!"

Julia bit on her lip hard to keep from making a sound.

"Right at me...it's coming too fast. The sound, the terrible screech! Yes, here are the fears. Oh, my children, what will they do now? And our new daughter, never a chance! Who will care for the boys, Jim doesn't really know how..."

Alina paused, and the pause lengthened. Her young head bowed on the young body.

"And then?" asked Reverend Matthews softly.

Alina lifted her head, breathing deeply, a mother's pain evident in her eyes. "Well, then? Why blackness, of course. There was no pain, you know, just that sudden blackness. Until...until the windy song came back to me." Her brow furrowed, a small confusion passing through her eyes. "Yes, the windy song. I used to sing that song to Jimmy J. and little David, you know. My mother, from back then, taught it to me. It was from her mother before that and way beyond that from the Indians who used to be here before. It's really an old Indian song. That's why it doesn't have any particular words. It's just a song that is chanted in the evenings to please the windy spirits. Maybe the settlers once had the Indian words, but not anymore." Alina sighed and then smiled, her eyes clear, her memories now painless, a radiance glowing from her. The thrall of the moment bound the minds of all watching her.

"I think we need more wood on the fire, Richard," Julia said, her words finally breaking the penetrating aurora of timelessness.

"Yes, yes," Richard agreed softly.

"You see, Daddy?" asked Alina, her voice suddenly her own again, "*do you see, Daddy? Why I must go to them!*"

Richard looked at her, in pain, and tears came from his eyes. "Go where, Alina? Where would we go, even if we could?"

"Why, to 210 Yale Street, of course. Up in Lincoln. That's where Jim and I lived."

"But how do you know they are still there?" Richard asked.

"You see, Richard," snorted Dr. Wollen, "you see how a powerful delusion can take hold of others. We really have to be very careful at this point."

"Oh, shut up, Wollen!" snarled Doc Thompson.

"Richard?" asked Reverend Matthews, "would you mind if I called telephone information up in Lincoln? Maybee..."

"By all means, Richard," agreed Wollen condescendingly. "Let's see if that is the correct place. Of course, it won't be, and then we can get on with the real business here."

"I...I," murmured Richard weakly, but it was too late, Reverend Matthews was already on the telephone.

"I got the operator," he indicated. "210 Yale Street, a Mr. Jim or probably James Hanks..." He smiled at Alina while he waited.

"Oh Daddy," Alina exclaimed excitedly. "I never thought of calling him up on the telephone."

"Aha," smiled Reverend Matthews. He hung up the receiver and wrote something on a piece of paper. "Here," he said, "is Jim Hanks' phone number...if you want it."

"Oh, Daddy," Alina immediately breathed, her eyes widening, "Do you think we should really call him up?"

"No! Definitely I do not." Richard said, regaining some of his firmness. "Why, what would we ever say to him? He would think we are totally crazy!"

"Oh, come on, Richard. She probably looked up his number," Wollen began.

"Yes," said Alina, ignoring Wollen. "He would get scared and upset, too. Jim always gets upset easily. After he came back from Korea, you know. He was always nervous after that."

"You see how delusions can suck people into them?" said Wollen.

"Alina, darling," Julia said, ignoring Wollen. "It's

really way past your bedtime. Don't you think we can talk more about this in the morning?"

"Yes, Mama. I suppose so." She hugged her mother, and then continued: "Haven't you heard Little Richard whimpering upstairs? You haven't paid him any attention at all."

"Oh, for heaven's sake," Julia stammered, "why I haven't heard a thing except your...your..."

"That's all right, Mama. We can talk about that tomorrow."

Chapter
EIGHTEEN

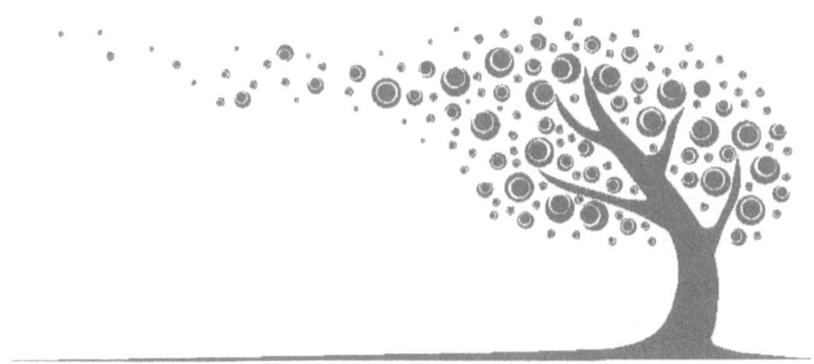

Richard watched his wife and daughter leave the room, their arms entwined. "You know, Doc Thompson," he began, now speaking instinctively to the old familiar physician, "I've never seen them so close, so equal. Usually, Julia has treated little Alina, well, rather distantly."

"And you?" Thompson asked knowingly. Richard avoided Thompson's implication. "How do you explain," he asked instead, "that, well, that weird change in her voice?"

Wollen broke in. "Hysterical children often can imitate a power figure, someone who has undue influence over them at a subconscious level. Compulsive imitations like this are not uncommon..."

"Really, Wollen," Thompson snorted, "you are becoming quite tedious. How can you witness..."

"I *am* a man of science, Thompson!" said Wollen savagely. "Not a *witness* to anything at all, not a witness to something other than a mental derangement in a young girl, probably a passing and curable one. What are witnesses, anyway? Except irrational, Impressionable personalities, helplessly searching for supports in life. No! Leave witnesses to the simple minded. Men of science must not trust what they witness, they must always remain rational and reasonable and submit what they think they witness to tests and research."

Doc Thompson was about to give his retort to this argument but instead simply offered: "Oh, bother!" He turned to Richard. "I know that you will object of course, but why don't the young and courageous Reverend here, and I, make an effort to contact this Jim Hanks up in Lincoln?"

"I really don't want to carry this any further," Richard began.

"But what an opportunity, Richard," Reverend Matthews said, his eyes wide, almost pleading. "Heavens, there are many children, especially in India, where reincarnation is expected, and in the Middle East, and even in Alaska among the Tlingit peoples, there are many children who remember. So why not here in Nebraska, here in the United States. Yes! Please allow us to go and call on this man. If, indeed, he had two children, a wife who died, let us try to arrange a meeting..."

"I couldn't possibly...why he'd laugh us out of town."

"How absurd," Wollen said thinly. "I'm amazed at all this! Why, you gentlemen actually wish to plunge this unfortunate child *deeper* into her delusion rather than extricate her from it. This is a level of irresponsibility..."

"But what if it is true?" asked Reverend Matthews, simply.

"Impossible! Utterly impossible!" Wollen's voice had risen to a near shout.

"Well, Richard," smiled Doc Thompson in triumph. "Whether or not you consent, I, at least, am going to go talk to this man up in Lincoln."

"And I, also," agreed Matthews with determination.

"Richard," Wollen stuttered, "no psychiatrist could even hope to affect a recovery under circumstances like these. If you agree to this, well, to this totally irrational approach...well, I'll just have to send you my bill for this consultation here. I have real matters that deserve my attention."

Richard gazed past Dr. Wollen. Outside, the wind seemed to accompany the melody that had begun drifting down from upstairs. He was silent for a moment, then he sighed. "Yes, Doctor Wollen, perhaps you had better just send the bill along."

Chapter
NINETEEN

It seemed their daughter held in her a woman's memories, yet these from another time and from another place, although not too far in the past or too far distant in place. For the city of Lincoln, if there the truth of the memories was to be found or not, was no more than two hours away by car. These older memories in their daughter were held alongside or behind those she otherwise held of her own self since her birth, and that these older memories indeed induced confusion there could be no doubt; but, too, they now realized, they the two parents, that it was not their daughter who was confused, but they themselves.

The two parents now also realized, perhaps only in wordless ways, that in front of the older memories their daughter would remain their daughter whether the memories were true ones or false ones.

When all the visitors had left the old farmhouse, when the fireplace ashes had turned grey, and the bourbon bottle, nearly empty now, had been put back in place, finally Richard's settled into quietness for the night. He climbed into the wide bed next to Julia, who laid there rigidly for a moment.

"Have I," he whispered, "really been...uh, not passionate..."

Julia smiled coyly over at him. "Oh, I don't know. I haven't had many other men for comparison."

"Many? What do you mean many?"

"Silly Daddy," Julia said, imitating her daughter. She snuggled closer to Richard who gathered her into his arms.

"I've always loved you, you know, in my way."

Julia didn't respond, but sighed and said contentedly: "We are too old now for passion anyway. I'm content that we've been a match for each other, a good match...and I've never wanted anyone else."

Richard bit his lip to stifle his tears. "I am going to let Alina go up to Lincoln, I'm going to let her have this wish of hers, that is if that man will speak to us."

"Oh, Rich, I'm so glad! I don't know what all this means, I just don't know. But I feel that it, well, it's somehow the right thing to do."

"Maybe, maybe not," Richard mused. "Anyway, Thompson and Matthews are going to try to arrange this. I can't imagine what that Jim Hanks will say about it all...If Hanks will agree to see us, I've asked Matthews and Doc not to tell us or Alina anything about him. Let Alina find out fresh what's to be found out. Julia, let me be pragmatic just this little bit. I don't what to test her or anything like that. But if she was this...Helena, well then she ought to know the facts herself. So let's don't prompt her on anything."

Julia's voice quivered. "There is something in Alina, something about her. But, somehow...well, it *is* frightening, and I've got to admit that. But, somehow, I know she's going to come through this."

"I can only hope so," Richard said softly, his lips on Julia's forehead. "But I hope I never have another day and night like this, never, for the rest of my life."

"It's her problem, Rich, and it *will* be all right."

His lips had snuggled into her neck. "Whatever quality my passion has been, I'd really like to give you some of it right now…"

Julia grinned, reached over, and turned out the light, and they knew they were better together now.

Chapter
TWENTY

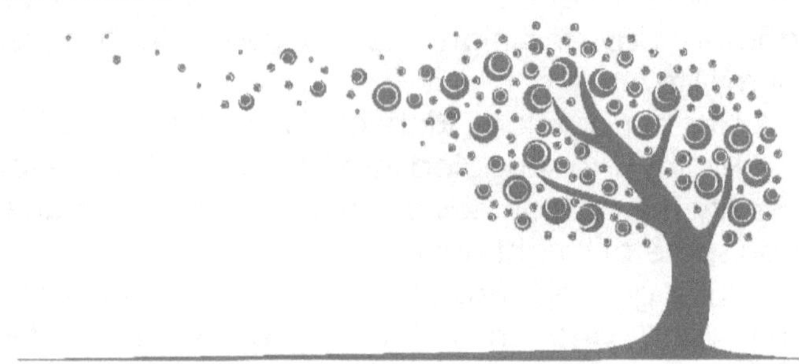

The ride up to Lincoln was a quiet one. At its start, Richard had said to Thompson and Matthews: "Now, don't tell us anything about Jim Hanks as we agreed."

Doc had said: "Well, there's nothing to tell, anyway. Hanks listened to us. He was quiet, but then said he'd talk to his two sons about it. Then he called back two days later and said that we could come. So that's all we know, which is nothing." Since then no one had said very much. Alina was comfortably, if tightly, settled between Reverend Matthews and Doc Thompson in the back seat. The weather along the highway was grey and a light snow fell here and there.

After a while, Doc Thompson said, "I've had children, yes, and some grownups, too, come to me in the past with similar stories, and this will be the first anybody ever checked out. If this is verified, it will be the first time. For me it will make history."

"In my calling, uh, profession," began Reverend Matthews, "we are not really taught how to deal with situations like this. Questions as to the before and the hereafter are readily turned aside, or explained away. But other cases *have* been checked out, Doc, and with some amazing results."

Richard grunted from the driver's seat. "I don't think, even if this does check out, that I'll permit an official case to be made out of this, either for science or religion."

"I don't think we were intimating anything of the sort, Richard," Thompson said calmly. "Merely that if this does check out, it would give me a deep personal satisfaction."

"He means just knowing there is more to life than just living it, and then dying, Richard," Julia advised.

"You know," Richard said as they reached the outskirts of Lincoln, "afterwards, after we meet these Hankses, then what? Are we supposed to change our lives somehow? Are we supposed to make two families into one, just because Helena was his wife, and Alina is now our daughter?"

"Isn't it a coincidence," sighed Julia, "that Helena and Alina are names so much alike. How do you suppose that came about?"

"Really, Julia," worried Richard, who himself was very nervous, "let's don't add yet another mystery to all this."

"All due respects to keeping Alina and your family's anonymity," Reverend Matthews said, "but there are many researchers who in the future would be deeply appreciative of knowing about a case so clear cut as this one."

"It's *not* clear cut," Richard retorted, "at least not yet, and it might not ever be."

"Perhaps we might discuss all this at some other time, Reverend," Julia suggested. "It's all beside the point at this moment. I would agree with Richard. I wouldn't want Alina or our family becoming a laughingstock or a side-show."

"You're quite right, Julia," Matthews agreed.

But Alina whispered loud enough so that Doc could hear: "I'll talk to you in private about anything you want to know. But I don't think either Mama or Daddy could stand all this if it continued too long. All I really want to do is see the two boys."

"And then?" whispered Reverend Matthews back.

"Why, there is no *then*, is there," she replied, looking around as they drove into Lincoln. She added, "there's only what *was*."

Richard steered the car through the expanse that Lincoln had become. No one spoke.

After a time, Alina the broke the calm: "Oh," she sighed. "It's grown so much since I saw it in that before. I don't think there were so many big buildings then, and no big freeways. But I might not be remembering everything."

No one commented on that.

They all became more tense as Richard finally located and drove down Yale Street. When he came to the one numbered 210 and parked in the driveway, Alina's face suddenly flushed. "Look," she pointed to the fruit trees in the yard and around the house, mostly bare of their leaves, their sap withdrawn for the winter. "Ooooh," she groaned, "look at the trees! They've grown so *tall* and *big*." Then, before anyone could stop her, she ran down the walk toward the door of the house, and there she began unthinkingly to turn the knob, hesitated, looking with embarrassment at the group following her.

"Oh, I nearly forgot," she giggled. "I don't live here anymore, do I? I should ring the bell, shouldn't I?"

"I think that would only be proper," agreed

Julia, smiling nervously.

The door opened in response to the bell. Alina looked at the tall woman who answered it. The woman looked back at her visitors.

It was the woman who broke the silence. "Oh, do forgive me," she blustered. "I'm Betty Hanks. I'm so sorry to stare. It's just that this is all so strange..."

Alina simply brushed past Betty Hanks into the house. Inside, she drew up at the foot of the stairs.

"Alina, really!" said Julia, catching up with her. "This is no way to behave."

"I'm so sorry, Mama, but I'm so excited," she retorted, looking around eagerly. "These walls are a *different* color, and there's a new rug." She turned to Betty. "You've *changed* everything! It used to be a peach color."

"Alina!" scolded Julia. "After all, this is *her* house."

"Oh, yes," agreed Alina.

"I'm dreadfully sorry, Mrs. Hanks," Julia apologized. "We...I don't know what to say..."

"Yes," agreed Betty, "but don't apologize. I don't know what to say, either. I've changed the entry several times. The years do come and go, and things simply wear out. When I first married Jim, well it *was* a nice peach color with a russet rug..."

"See, Mama. I told you so!"

"All right, Alina, you did. But we have to be polite here. After all, we have to be grateful for the forbearance of these people. This *must be* very strange for them."

Alina pursed her lips, then apologized. "I'm sorry, Mrs. Hanks. I suppose I'm taking a lot for granted." Her voice had deepened, the strange maturity beginning to possess her again.

"Yes, why, yes, it *is* strange," Mrs. Hanks said, uneasily stunned by the young girl's sudden shift of poise.

"May I see Jim now?" Alina asked.

"Yes, he's waiting in the living room with the two boys. It's this way." But Alina didn't wait for direction. She turned sharply and went to the left of the foyer, then down a hall toward the back of the house. The group followed wordlessly, except that Mrs. Hanks explained: "For some strange reason, whoever first built this house put the living room at the back."

The three men in the living room had risen, having overheard parts of the conversation from the foyer.

Alina looked at each of them intently, the smallness of her young body only accentuating the womanly bearing that once again had come over her. "Well, Jim," she finally said, "I'm sure this is incomprehensible to you." Her voice was full, resonate.

Jim Hanks stared at her wordlessly. He was a tall man, once muscular, but turning softly heavy with his years. His black hair was peppered with grey. "You've aged well enough, I see," Alina continued, "I'd like to hug you, but I suppose I shouldn't."

Jim Hanks stared down at her. "But you've got grey eyes. No one mentioned that..."

"Is that important?" Reverend Matthews asked.

"Of course it is, silly Reverend," said Alina, reverting momentarily to her young self. "Helena had grey eyes, too."

The room was then silent. Finally, Richard stepped forward and introduced himself. "I appreciate you letting us come...none of us know what to think about all this...here's my wife, Julia, and this is Doctor Thompson and Reverend Matthews."

After these introductions were done, no one knew what to do next.

"Might I sit down," asked Alina with her *other* voice. The older of the two young men jumped and produced a chair for her. Betty apologized for not having asked them to sit before. "Your daughter...well, she seems so mature, so strangely so."

Julia smiled. "It seems so, but only when she is thinking of her other...uh...her other life."

"But do you believe that?" asked Betty.

"Quite frankly, Mrs. Hanks," said Julia, "I *have* begun to believe that it's so. It's hard to credit, but I don't see any other..."

"Now, come on!" said Jim Hanks. "You're talking about reincarnation, about something that's only, well, fiction. Nobody..."

Alina was oblivious to this conversation. Her eyes were fixed on those two young men, both of whom were clearly uncomfortable. They sat meekly in their chairs, allowing the girl to scrutinize them carefully. The silence quickly became unbearable.

"What does she want of us," began Jim Hanks.

Doc Thompson entered the silence. "Alina's recall seems extraordinarily clear, Mr. Hanks. If you would want to ask her any questions, she would probably oblige. As you see, she is exhibiting a sort of double personality. At the moment she seems to be more like an older woman with some strange memories. At other times, the times we prefer, she is our young Alina. We would hope she could satisfy the urges that seem to be remaining in, or coming out of, the old memories, and then to forget them permanently."

"I don't believe a *word* of this!" Jim Hanks said. "I'm just a working man, blue collar, a church-going man. We don't deal with things like this."

Alina turned to him. "Still belittling yourself, Jim?" she asked.

"What?" asked Hanks in surprise. He gazed silently at Alina, who waited silently, smiling. Then: "Helena was always teasing me about my low opinion of myself."

"Yes, that's true," agreed Alina. "But there was love in the teasing, wasn't there?"

"Why, yes. Always. Listen, if you are Helena, the way you claim, then you ought to know everything she and I did. Now, you go on and tell me some private things. Something no one else could know."

"I'll try, Jim. The memories come and go, and things aren't too clear at times..."

"Ah, so you *can't*..."

"Well, there's one thing," Alina began distantly. "Yes," she said then more directly, "did you ever find the medals?"

"The medals?" Hanks asked in anger. "What about them?"

"Why, the medals you got in Korea. The one's I hid away, because I was afraid Jimmy J. might get and swallow them. I bet you never found them, did you?"

"But Jim," Betty said, "we've looked everywhere for them after Helena died..."

"Well, anyone could have found out about that," Hanks growled.

"You never found them, did you?" Alina now giggled in pleasure. "Well, if you still got that old-fashioned sink upstairs in the bathroom, you go right up and look underneath and behind the hot water pipe, in that small hole you never filled in. I put the medals in there. They are wrapped in a piece of green silk."

The room was silent. Then the older of the two young men dashed out of the room and up the stairs.

"You can't possibly know..." Hanks began.

But the young man had quickly rushed back down the stairs and into the room. "Dad!" he gasped in disbelief, "here they are, green silk and all."

Jim Hanks closed his eyes. "Anyone could have found out we looked high and low for them, and put some old medals there. I don't even recognize these any more..."

"Of course you recognize them, Jim. You were very proud of them. But then there is the wound you got in Korea, that special wound you were so worried about, and never ever talked of to anyone else but me."

"Everyone knows I was wounded..."

"Yes, but there's that *one* on a very private part of you, that small piece of shrapnel that left a deep scar that never filled in and that worried you more than all the rest of the wounds. The one you first felt might deprive you..."

"Oh!" Hanks said, with a great outburst of air, his face blushing.

"Do *you* remember my two miscarriages between Jimmy J. and David, the fact that you said perhaps it was for the best because your salary wasn't big enough..."

"Oh, my God I" moaned Hanks.

"Alina!" admonished Julia, her voice shaking.

Alina went on, heartlessly almost. "You always wanted to be a forest ranger, but the Korean war came along and you got drafted. You were drafted, and you hated it, and you lost your chance to go to forestry school on a scholarship."

Jim Hanks' face had become immobile, frozen as if the coldest of winds from an unknown void had touched him. He stared at Alina, but as if seeing right through her to some figure no one else could see.

"And, Jim Hanks, the fact that we both knew I was pregnant again, only you and I and before I even went to the doctor, and you were on top of the world at the chance of having a daughter when..."

"*I couldn't help it*!" screamed Hanks, rising to his feet, his face red with anger. "I couldn't *help* it; I didn't see the other car!" He towered over Alina, as if to strike her. Richard rose to interfere, the two boys shrank into the couch, and Julia let out a little scream.

But Alina looked calmly up at him. "Don't grieve anymore, Jim, soldier Jim. Even I didn't see the car until the very last moment, when I turned my head and it hit the side of the Pontiac."

Hanks looked down at her, his face blanching. He fell to his knees before her, his face level with hers, his eyes staring into the grey depths of her own. "Why...you called me soldier boy, you only did that when I was in the VA hospital...getting back on my feet."

"Yes, and you used to get so angry. Right then, soldiering was the last thing you ever wanted to hear of again. But you always felt better after you'd been a little angry about something, about anything."

The room was utterly silent. Jim Hanks' face was relaxed and suddenly tender. Is it possible...?"

"Have you grieved all these years, Jim, you know, about the car accident?"

"Of course I have. Down deep. I've blamed myself; I should have been more careful."

"There's no need anymore, you know."

"I was so alone without you, so very alone, lost..."

They stared into each other's eyes. Alina's posture, her manner, her deep empathy for the man before her, now almost completely erased the *young* Alina. She appeared larger, grown, mature, a woman. Julia and Richard stopped breathing. Alina allowed the moment to ripen, to fulfill itself as a knowledgeable woman would. When the emotion had peaked, and the understanding had come, then she said: "I'm so happy that you found another, so very, very glad for you both."

"Yes, we've been good for each other, and the boys."

"Yes," said Alina. "And the boys."

Now the spectra of maturity slipped and vanished. The young Alina's face lit up. "Oh, the boys!"

"Yes, Alina," said Richard ever so softly, relieved that the eerily mature communion between his daughter and the older man had passed. "You said you wanted to make sure the boys were all right. Well, here they are."

"*Not* true, silly Daddy," Alina said, her voice worried. "I've been studying them very closely. The oldest boy here, the one with the pale blue eyes and blond hair, well he is clearly little David."

The young man smiled nervously and blushed. "I can see he's grown up fine, just as I knew he would. I bet he gets excellent grades in college! Yes, well, he must be just about to enter college now."

Then Alina paused. "But this other young

man," she observed, her voice becoming unsteady. "I don't believe I know him at all."

"Oh, Jim," breathed Betty, "she seems to know, she knows…"

"Knows what, Mrs. Hanks?" asked Richard.

Hanks had risen slowly to his feet, then sat back down in the armchair. He put his hand over his eyes. In a moment he removed it, and looked at them all. "Well, we wanted to make sure, so we didn't tell you something."

"You mean you tried to trick us?" Richard asked, his voice rising.

"Easy, Richard," warned Reverend Matthews. "That would only be natural."

"No, not *trick* you, exactly, just something we didn't think you ought to be told at first, because it didn't seem important when we thought all this was a farce of some kind."

The room was silent. Hanks continued. "This here is our son John, who is David's half-brother. Betty's and my son. He was born after Helena…well, you know."

"Oh," said Alina softly. "But then, where is Jimmy J?"

Jim Hanks hung his head in silence.

"Where *is* he, Jim?" said Alina. "Where *is* my son?"

"Well, Helena…uh, Alina…I don't know what to call you."

"Alina will do," she advised him, maturity overlaying her youth once more.

"Well, Jimmy J, he was restless, you see, and went off and joined the Marines. To see the world, he said. He loved it. We got lots of his letters still…maybe you'd like to read them…?" Hanks tried to smile.

"But where is he *now*, Jim?" Alina demanded,

her eyes wide with incomprehension.

"He was in Viet Nam, Helena, uh Alina."

"In Viet Nam?"

"Yes."

Alina stared at him, then turned to her mother. The air of adulthood fell away, leaving the little girl visible once again. She turned helplessly to Julia. "Oh, Mama! Is that where the war was?"

Jim Hanks answered. "Jimmy J was killed in action a few months ago, just a few days before the war ended. One of the last to die. The War Department said he died with great valor, and saved the lives of many other boys by his action. They've already sent a posthumous medal, the Bronze Star."

Alina had ceased to hear him. She looked at Julia, her face drawn with deep pain, and then she looked at Richard: "Oh, Mama, Daddy!" she wailed, "My son is dead!"

Julia tried to reach her in time, but Alina slipped unconsciously to the floor before anyone else could move.

Chapter
TWENTY-ONE

The next day dawned clear and brilliant. A warmth in the air returned, and when Alina awoke, she knew it would be almost warm enough outside to be without a coat, but just. Mama would make her bundle up anyway, of course. But she was not eager to get up. Instead, she lay in the bed, warm and serene. She had slept without a dream at all, a merciful blackness without a tremor of an inward, unwanted image disturbing her. She barely remembered the car ride home. Mama had driven all the way herself, since Daddy had held her in his arms the entire trip, and even had sat with her long after she slept. She had briefly awakened once, to find him still there, near where she could touch him if she had wanted to.

Lying warm, now, in the bed on this new morning, she felt a little empty, but not so very empty that the smell of biscuits drifting up the stairs was of no interest. Her stomach growled and her mouth watered. Amazing, she thought, especially after all that from yesterday.

The shock of loss had been tremendous. But it seemed as if it had gone as fast as it had come. Aunt Margaret often said that children get over things faster than grownups. But, too, she felt content in some other way, something she couldn't quite figure out, but which lay just in reach of understanding, yet hadn't come clear yet.

She thought over this for a while, twisting luxuriously in the soft bed. It won't be long, she told herself, before all the dolls and the panda bear lamp will have to go. Something a bit more feminine, more grown up. She decided to discuss the redecoration problem with Oakley, who would be bursting in through the kitchen door before long, as usual screaming to run around outside.

She dressed slowly, thoughts crossing her mind, suddenly dissatisfied with all her clothes. To immature, all of them. Daddy yelled whenever she wanted anything new. What would he say about a whole lot of all new things?

When she finally did get herself down the stairs to the breakfast alcove, she was surprised to find Aunt Margaret there. "Goodness," she said, kissing her parents as usual, "there must be something special going on. Aunt Margaret has *never* been here for breakfast."

"Nor, in fact," Daddy said sheepishly, "hardly ever for dinner, either. But that's going to change, now."

"Your Daddy was kind enough to tell me everything that happened last night," Margaret said.

"I *wanted* to tell Aunt Margaret, myself," Richard began, clearing his throat, "at a time when you were here also, Alina, that I've been unkind to her. I've waited for you to come down so you could hear it. I hope she will forgive me. I'm bound to be difficult, of course," he grinned with embarrassment. "But if we both…try."

Julia stopped eating her pancakes and looked at Richard with sudden tears.

"Mama," Alina said, in a grown-up voice, "you simply have to stop crying over *everything*!"

"It runs in my side of the family, Alina," smiled Julia.

"Why Richard. I never thought you were particularly unkind to me," said Margaret, "just to yourself."

"But I have been. I've been pretty noisy sometimes about your being…well, odd." He smiled hopefully.

"But that's true. I am. Don't you have to be to stay at least a little happy?"

"Really, Margaret," Julia smiled, "a little sensible, too, helps a lot."

"Well, at any rate, I want you to be closer to us from now on," Richard said. "After all, you and Alina seem to speak the same language, and you'll be good for her, maybe for us, too…me, too. I have it in mind that you might come and live with us. Why should you stay all alone in that huge house?"

"Well, Richard. I *am* impressed, now. But I could never leave my house. There are too many things and memories in it I'd miss."

Richard shrugged his shoulders. "And you, Alina, well I think I'll start over with you, too."

Alina gazed beamingly at her Daddy. "Great!" she said. "I'd like to have some new more grown-up clothes."

"You got them."

"A whole new wardrobe." Her eyes were big. "Why not?"

"Richard, really! Her clothes are perfectly good," Julia said, but she was smiling.

"Wow," Alina said. "And I'd like some new lamps and some bookshelves, and wow! Am I ever hungry."

"Well, there's plenty of food here," said Julia, pushing the pancakes, biscuits, and bacon onto her daughter's plate.

"Wow, young lady, am I hungry, too," Richard said, grinning at her. They all ate in silence for a few moments. Richard kept his eyes on Alina. There were words on the top of his tongue. He didn't know whether to speak them or not. He decided to let them out: "Well, silly young lady, what do we do next?"

Alina looked at him and smiled. "Oh, I don't know, Daddy. Aunt Margaret says that time heals everything. Do you suppose that's true?"

"I think it might possibly be true," Richard agreed.

"Then let's let some time go by, and see."

Richard didn't say anything, but his eyes shone with pride.

"Margaret?" Julia said changing the subject, "I was wondering where Alina's grey eyes might have come from. Do you know?"

"Well, of course I do. My mother told me that her mother said that *her* mother had big grey eyes. They run somewhere in our family."

"You know," Richard reminded, "the Hanks family is coming down to dinner tonight, and Reverend Matthews and Doc, too. The Hanks want to see more of you. It seems the two boys are simply fascinated by all this."

Alina smiled. "David has grown up fine, hasn't he? Mrs. Hanks has been a good mother to him."

"Yes," Julia said. "It all seems to have worked out for them."

"Well, I'll be glad if they are wanting to come.

I'll enjoy watching David. He was quite young, you know, when…but let's not talk of that anymore."

"You know, Alina," Julia said, "Mr. Hanks gave you Jimmy J's Bronze Star medal. He thought you might like to keep it."

"Oh?" asked Alina. She paled for a moment, then stood up and began to smile. The smile widened to a grin. Finally, she started laughing.

The three adults were taken back, Julia started a worried frown.

"Alina?" Richard asked.

"It's nothing, Daddy, nothing. Something I just remembered…just realized."

"Whatever is it?" Julia asked.

"Nothing. Nothing at all," she lied. "If I leave now, I can meet Oakley halfway, and I bet I'll beat her in our usual race across the field to the old cow pond."

"Well, you better bundle up, and eat a bit more. If you're going to keep up with that tomboy, you need more food," said Julia smiling.

"Silly Mama," Alina giggled, gobbling her food. "Oakley isn't a real tomboy. She only pretends she is."

A few moments later, the hearty breakfast warming her stomach, Alina dashed out toward Oakley's house. Oakley rushed out, too, and then the two girls were running, shouting, across the frozen field.

Chapter
TWENTY-TWO

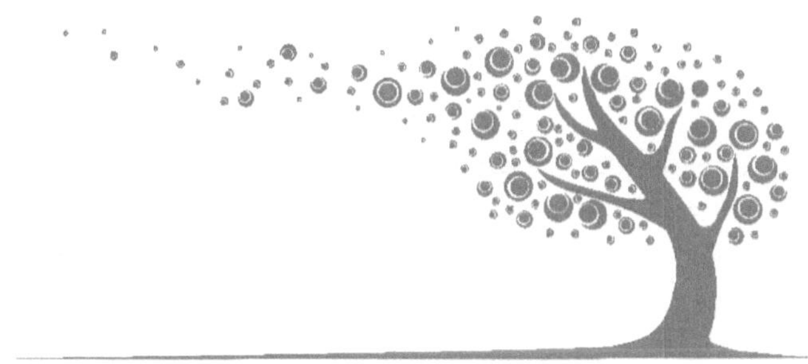

That night, after the delicious, comfortable dinner with the Hanks family, and those good souls Matthews and Thompson, Alina got herself ready for bed. Down the hall Little Richard was whimpering away, as usual a squalling outburst now and then.

Julia was still downstairs, and Alina knew that before long, if Little Richard wasn't soothed, he would break into full-fledged squalling. She took the Bronze Star from the drawer where she had placed it, and went to the nursery.

She placed the large gold disk, dangling from its silk ribbon, around his neck. His small eyes watched her with fixed interest.

"You know," she said softly, "I feel as if I've lived through a whole life, and have begun a new one just like you. But I guess you can't understand…perhaps you can somewhere inside you."

The baby gurgled up at her. "I remember your whimpering, you know…"

She looked down at him with a deep love. "That ugly, stupid war is over now," she continued even more softly. "You needn't be afraid of that anymore." There was no answer. "But I suppose," she sighed, "you're really too young to remember anything yet," she whispered.

"But I'll sing you the windy song one last time. After all, you're not Jimmy J anymore, but Little Richard. You're Mama's son now, not mine."

Downstairs Richard and Julia looked upward as the lilting lullaby wafted like a light breeze through the house. Mutely they joined hands and tiptoed up to the nursery, watching their daughter sing to the infant. Alina hung over the crib, her body soft and sturdy beneath the flannel nightgown.

The windy song ended and drifted away. Little Richard was soundly asleep.

"Thank you, Alina," Julia said quietly. "But we'd better take the ribbon away. He might choke on it."

"Yes, I wasn't going to leave it," Alina told her. "But you put it away someplace for him. He may want it some time."

"I don't understand," Julia said softly. "Are you giving the medal to the baby?" asked Richard.

"Silly Daddy, don't you understand?"

"No, not really."

Alina smiled sadly. "It *belongs* to him, Daddy. He earned it with doing something brave in a stupid war." Richard and Julia were very silent. Alina looked at them. "But let's never tell him, unless, of course, he asks."

"We certainly won't," said Julia, her eyes gleaming with sudden understanding.

Richard was still confused. "What is going on?" he whispered. "Silly Daddy, go talk to Aunt Margaret," Alina said fondly. "She, much better than I can, she'll tell you that love brings all of us together time and again even if in different ways."

Postlude

This universe of infinities sonorously sings through
the mind at intervals, sufficient enough at least
that a memory of it, a yearning towards it, is
never fully erased, never fully suppressed.

In this way, then, in a prairie place where the winds come and go, and in different directions, did the young girl babe whose birth was at first fretful become a young girl and know herself also a woman before her natural time to do so, and she knew this womanhood from her soul's time before. None of this was talked of very much, and so these events came and went like the various winds which come and go from and to no one knows where.

But among these various winds are the currents of love which blow, too, in the realms of souls. And these currents, like a song to those who can hear them, link together those souls who truly love each other, even though no one knows why or how.

Many in themselves know and understand this, of course, and know as much whether they speak or tell of it or not.

A BIOMIND SUPERPOWERS BOOK FROM
SWANN-RYDER PRODUCTIONS, LLC

www.ingoswann.com

Other Books by Ingo Swann

Everybody's Guide to Natural ESP
Master of Harmlessness
Penetration
Penetration: Special Edition Updated
Preserving the Psychic Child
Psychic Literacy
Psychic Sexuality
Purple Fables
Reality Boxes
Resurrecting the Mysterious
Secrets of Power, Volume 1
Secrets of Power, Volume 2
Star Fire
The Great Apparitions of Mary
The Wisdom Category
Your Nostradamus Factor